# The Sorcerer's Quest

## The Sorcerer's Saga Book 1

### Rain Oxford

ISBN: 1530253756
ISBN-13: 978-1530253753

# CONTENTS

# CHAPTER 1

"Please just let me tell you---" I stopped because I was suddenly talking to a door. I sighed and started back down the road. Dread and hunger were wearing on me. A man stepped out of the forest, followed by a huge, overweight, slow-moving animal with black and white spots. "Excuse me, sir," I said, giving him as much excitement as I could muster up.

"Yes? How can I help you?" he asked. He was a kind looking man and although he wore shabby clothes, his face and hair were clean.

"I was wondering, would you be interested in buying some magic beans?"

He frowned and shook his head. "Sorry, I've just traded my own magic beans for this beast." He indicated the animal, which was eating the grass. "I would be willing to trade the beast for your beans, though. I really don't think I got the fair end of that deal."

I pulled out the handful of beans from my pocket and studied the beast. "I… I'm sorry. My mother would kill me if I did." That was a lie, but I couldn't live with myself if I subjected an animal to her.

"I understand. Good day to you."

"And you." He hurried on his way and I sighed. *At least he didn't notice my family seal embossed on my dark green robe.* That might have been due to the fact that I had my robe inside out. This was on purpose.

After the fifth door I knocked on where nobody answered, I had reversed the robe to hide the gold needlework. It worked; people answered the door only to slam it in my face. Still, it was better to appear as an idiot than a member of the Dracre family. Dracre was a name people feared even speaking aloud and nobody was foolish enough to open the door to us. My mother in particular was known as the most vindictive sorceress of all, a title which she boasted every time I screwed up.

And I screwed up an awful lot. For example, all I had to do was sell some cursed beans. I spent three days traveling the land, scouring every hill and valley for some poor fellow who would buy them, but the only people who would even open the door were in fact, poor. It wasn't that my family needed money; there was never a shortage of people who needed curses and potions. My mother just wanted to make sure I was doing my part in spreading mayhem.

I sat down on a large boulder beside the road. My feet hurt. The unfortunate truth was that I should have been able to sell the beans to someone, but I was a very lousy sorcerer. I pulled out a lump of clay and my wand.

It was a perfectly straight wand made of rose with elegant sigils engraved in the handle. My mc threw away my first three wands and made me m...e proper sorcerer ones, like hers. Her wand was sinister and twisted, made of ebony with powerful carvings all over it that moved randomly. Unfortunately, no matter how much I tried to make one like hers, it just transformed into this every time I used it. It was a source of great amusement for my six older brothers.

Standing, I tossed my robe aside, both in shame and because it was a hot summer day. I carefully set the clay down on the rock and waved my wand at it, trying very hard to transform the mass into a hunk of bloody steak. Instead, energy shot through me, into my wand, and changed the clay into… an apple and broccoli. I groaned. *Why must I be a vegetarian?* All my brothers could conjure meat. I had to rely on hunting for meat, but every time I attempted it, I couldn't bring myself to shoot an animal.

"You shouldn't have that, young man," a voice startled me from my misery. I looked up and saw a man with a nice, beige shirt and blue slacks. From the decent condition of his clothes and his well-styled brown hair, I knew he was a traveling salesman. They had all the best possessions. He pointed to my robe, on which the family crest was very clearly displayed.

"It's my family's mark," I said, trying to sound fierce.

He frowned at me with disbelief, undoubtedly due to my blond hair and blue eyes. Every Dracre had black hair and burgundy eyes. "That is the Dracre crest, and I know they don't have any wizards."

I flinched. "I'm not a wizard! I'm a sorcerer!"

The man scoffed. "With blond hair? Impossible." He left, shaking his head and muttering about wizards trying to be what they weren't.

I sighed. My brothers teased me every day, saying things like that Mother stole me from a wizard family, or worse— a mage! Wizards were as anti-black-magic as they could get, whereas no decent sorcerers would ever lift a finger to help another person. The only people my family considered worse than wizards were mages, which were healers and quest makers.

Because wizards were known for their blond hair and all sorcerers had black hair, I would never be accepted into my family. I ate my apple and broccoli, then sighed and started heading home.

*     *     *

I arrived at a dark shack in the middle of the forest right at sunset. It was made of gray stone and covered in blood-colored ivy. The trees all around it were dead, which warned anyone passing by that it was a house of dark magic users. I tried to open the door, but it was locked. I sighed and knocked.

"Mother? I'm back." When there was no answer, I pulled out my wand and waved it at the door handle. The metal answered with a harsh burst of energy that burned my hand.

The door opened to my oldest brother. Zeustrum sneered, making his sharp, angular features stand out more than usual. "I *knew* you were a wizard."

"Get out of my way," I said.

"Say please, wizard."

"Move!" I yelled. His black hair was braided down his back, as usual. He was so proud of his hair that he never once cut it. I wanted to cut it short and watch him cry. When I was little and he tried to practice his torturing methods on me, I could only get him to leave me alone by pulling on his braid. Alas, he had learned my tricks, so I wouldn't even risk it this time.

He just smirked. "Mother said that if you didn't sell the cursed beans, you were not allowed in."

"It's not my fault! You have no idea how hard it is to sell magic produce these days."

"You are such a disappointment to the family," he said before shutting the door in my face. I waited a moment before turning the knob and entering.

The inside of the house was easily ten times the size of the outside. The kitchen was the heart of the house with the communal area circling it. Only a knee-high stone partition separated the kitchen and the living space around it. The partition also served as a very long table on which we prepared the ingredients for the potions. There were many pots, stirrers, and measuring tools that my family used to make poisons, potions, and curses.

The living area was mostly used for entertaining guests and planning. When wizards no longer offered curses, the Dracre family had a huge surge in clientele. On the north end, a winding staircase led to the second floor, where our bedrooms were. I headed for the stairs, only to hit what felt like a solid wall.

"Ayden, Zeus said you failed at the easy assignment I gave you," my mother's voice came from the kitchen. I hadn't seen her when I came in, but I should have known better.

"Good evening, Mother. I wouldn't say I failed exactly. Did I get money for them, no, but it was because--_"

"Did you give them away?" she asked.

"No."

She was a very tall and thin woman with straight black hair, cold burgundy eyes, and prominent cheekbones. There was nothing gentle or warm about her appearance. Even her long nails looked more like claws than the flat nails that other people had. I knew from experience that they were very painful.

"Go to your room. I will deal with you in the morning." Her voice was soft, which was as feminine as it got and told me without a shadow of doubt that I was in serious trouble. If I had given them away, at least I would have accomplished her goal of brewing chaos.

I ran up the stairs, down the circular hall to the last door, and shut myself in my bedroom. My room was the smallest in the house— barely large enough for my small bed. I pulled the storage chest out from under the low bed and changed my black shirt and pants for a more comfortable, short-sleeved tan shirt and brown pants.

There was a reason I didn't have a mirror in my room; as if being the only one in my family who didn't enjoy causing chaos wasn't embarrassing enough, I was also the runt. Along with my blond hair and blue eyes, I was small and thin for my age. As I started to roll up my robe, I heard several of my brothers talking outside my door.

"Do you think Mother will finally kick him out?" Thaddeus, my youngest older brother asked. Thad never instigated anything on his own, preferring to stand back and let everyone else fight, then side with the winner. Basically, he followed Zeustrum around.

"I hope so. Maybe then we could get a brother who is worth something," Bevras said. He was my second oldest and easily the most violent. Zeustrum and Bevras were twins and always backed each other up.

"Mother would never let him go," Zeustrum argued. "She wouldn't let someone ruin our good name. I heard her telling father that this was his last chance. My guess is that she'll get rid of him for good."

*For good? Mother wouldn't . . .* Yes, she would.

"So he's not going with us to destroy Magnus?"

*Magnus?* Mother was sending them to defeat *Magnus?* The wizard was well-known throughout all Akadema for his great power and selflessness. Not even the most powerful sorcerers could get into his castle.

"Of course not. Ayden would never stand a chance against a wizard as powerful as him."

My heart sank as I realized what I had to do. I wasn't born cruel like my brothers and it was obvious I wasn't just going to grow into it. The only way I was going to be accepted by my family was to do something drastic. If I could practice by causing some mayhem along the way, all the better for my reputation.

I gathered everything I owned into a small bag and waited for it to become quiet again. Soon, I opened the door, found that my brothers were gone, and snuck down the hall. When I reached the bottom of the stairs, I hesitated, but I didn't see anyone. Sneaking out the front door was almost too easy.

I paused at a huge willow tree I used to hide in as a child and looked back at the house, certain this was a trap of some kind… but there was no one watching, waiting to stop me. Then I turned and jumped with a loud squeak. I slapped my hand over my mouth to hush myself. My father, who was standing right in front of me, just looked sort of sad. "Please don't tell Mother," I whispered. I would have cursed myself if I could for thinking I could escape my fate.

He put his finger to his lips in a gesture of silence. He did that sometimes when only I was around, and I always thought it was odd. My father wasn't like my mother. Yes, he was a sorcerer and therefore only used magic for selfish gains, but he was never cruel to me or my brothers. If I thought a sorcerer was capable of it, I would go as far as to say he felt sorry for me.

Although Kille Rynorm did not have bulky muscle like a warrior, he was much stronger than a normal sorcerer needed to be. His hair was black and short, adding to the severity of his face. His jaw was angular and always closely shaven. What people noticed first was his eyes, which changed colors, supposedly with his mood. They were usually a very dark rust color, but on this night they were gold.

He never raised his voice and never lost his temper. He didn't need to. When he was around, people just wanted to keep their head down and behave. Although I never met his family, I imagined they were the same.

His family were dragon trainers and extremely successful at it until my father married my mother. She tried to take over without any knowledge of dragons. After several were killed because of her improper treatment, they let the rest of the dragons go free. My mother often told me that dragons all went extinct before I was born, but I liked to think they were just hiding from her.

In their rooms.

Like I did.

Instead of letting his hand fall to his side, he set it gently on my shoulder. "I'm not going to tell your mother. You should have left ages ago."

"Zeus said that Mother will get rid of me. Does she plan to kill me?"

"Yes. Your mother has always been far too ambitious. To her, children are akin to slaves. Run while you have the chance. I am not a seer, but I know you will learn so much on the journey you have ahead of you."

I nodded. "Will she be mad at you for letting me go?"

He smirked, which utterly shocked me. I didn't think my father was even capable of that. "I will deal with her. For today at least." His grin faded. "Eventually, she will come after you."

"Then I will prove myself to be the strongest sorcerer in Akadema before she does." As I started down the dark road, my resolve strengthened. I knew I could become such a powerful sorcerer that not even my brothers could dispute it. That, or I would never return.

\*     \*     \*

By the third day, I was regretting my decision. Akadema was a great place to live in a quiet village or alone in a cabin in the woods, but there wasn't much else. There were a few castles, yet even those were small. Basically, we had an abundance of forests, dirt roads, flat fields, and hills.

Although I passed plenty of travelers, none were interested in anything but trading and I had nothing of value. On the major roads, I normally passed four or five villages a day. Since they all looked the same, I could really have done with a change of scenery.

I was just about to turn back and head home when I heard a commotion from the right. There was some screaming and cries for help, so I decided to check it out. After all, there was always something a sorcerer could do to aggravate a problem.

I followed the dirt path over a hill, where I saw a quaint village in a shallow valley. Well, normally it was probably very pleasant. At the moment, though, it was on fire. When I saw men running around with their arms full of loot, I assumed that they were pillagers. "Well, if they're already being pillaged... the least I can do is get in on it." *Mother would be so proud if word got back to her that I terrorized an entire village.*

As I wandered into the town, I could easily tell the raiders apart from the residents by their forest-green cloaks. Mine was too clean to blend in, but after dropping it in the dirt and stomping on it a few times, it worked quite nicely. One of the looters passed me with a hefty bag of gold jewelry. I knew it contained jewelry because there was a hole in the bag that its contents spilled from.

I quickly gathered the wealth up and stuck it in my satchel. *Wow, that was easy.* The path was lined with small huts, so I picked the closest one. Before I could even step inside, though, a pillager came out and shoved a sack of loot into my arms.

"Oh, hello," he said. "When did you start?"

"Today," I answered automatically.

"Well, good to have you. Go lend Dorna a hand."

I hesitated. I wasn't supposed to be helping anyone. "Who's Dorna?" I asked. I wandered around the town and gathered up other loot that had been dropped. Unfortunately, it was nothing but food, wood carvings, and fancy cloths.

I heard a quiet nickering behind me, turned, and ducked quickly to avoid being skewered. A pure white unicorn with a pearlescent horn tossed his head and closed the distance between us. He sniffed at me and my robe as if looking for a treat, which made it very difficult to dodge his horn. I was in awe, really, but I was also perturbed. Unicorns were widely known to dislike sorcerers, so the fact that this one was acting like I was his favorite person did not bode well for my mission.

"Please go away," I whispered, desperately hoping no one saw me with him. When he turned and pranced off, exactly as I had asked, I felt disappointed. Unicorns were rare and beautiful, but I had an image to keep up.

Soon, I worried that I would never cause any trouble if I didn't get to it. *What's the first step in pillaging?* Well, the villagers outnumbered the raiders, but the thieves had swords and the residents didn't. A plan dawned on me.

I looked around for the closest object and picked a cluster of wildflowers. Then I pulled my wand out with my free hand and waved it at the bouquet. *Make these flowers like a sword.* Magic shot through the wand and into the flowers… but it didn't stop there. Sparkly blue energy jumped to the nearest sword and from that into another until every sword in the village changed into harmless flowers. My flowers remained just that.

*Oh, no.*

The raiders stared in shock at their colorful bouquets, as did the villagers. Then one resident made a cry of victory and all the thieves turned to run like their tails were on fire. Taking advantage, the residents chased them, waving their bread and rolls of cloth threateningly. I groaned when they all gathered around me.

They didn't look frightened. "You are the only wizard brave enough to help a humble town like this," one man said. Everyone else cheered with undue glee.

"Thank you, but I'm not a wizard; I'm a powerful and malevolent sorcerer."

The man frowned. "Oh… well, you were pretty frightening before you defeated the pillagers. You can yell at us a bit if it would help."

I shrugged. "No, I don't think there's much point now. However, it would be great if you could make it sound like I was part of the trouble. I'm trying to build a reputation."

He looked around at his own people and several of them nodded. "Certainly. We can tell everyone you led the pillagers. What is your name, young sir?"

"Ayden Dracre."

His complexion blanched. "Dracre is a well-known name in these parts, but we never knew they had a wizard— I mean a blond sorcerer. I wish we could offer you something in gratitude, but we have very little."

"I saw a pillager running off with a bag of gold jewelry," I pointed out.

"They were coming from the castle of Hershes. He brought it with him."

I nodded with understanding and pointed to the loaf of bread in his hand. "A meal would be nice then. I haven't actually eaten anything other than broccoli and apples in six days." Before I could say another word, I was directed to a hut, sat forcefully in a chair, and presented with more bread, soup, and roasted bird than I could eat.

I certainly tried, though. I ate until my stomach hurt, but when I tried to thank them and leave, they gave me another gift.

"This has been in our keep for many generations," the town's leader said, handing me a small treasure chest. It was made of dark wood and shiny silver metal with gold writing on the front side. Alas, I couldn't read it.

"What does this say? What's in it?" I asked.

"Only a wizard can read it and open it. A traveler lost it in a card game, but he told us it contained a creature of terrible power."

"That's very interesting. If I run across a wizard, maybe I can threaten him and make him open it."

The man frowned. "You could… just ask him nicely."

I ignored him. "Then I can use the creature to help me do my evil deeds. Why give it to me?"

"Well, we honestly don't want to keep it. There are too many women and children who fear that the monster will escape and even the bravest of our men say they hear the creature trying to get out."

After that, I was politely invited to leave and not return.

*　　*　　*

At nightfall, I went into the woods, gathered some fire kindle, and sat down on a thick tree root. I waved my wand at the pile, concentrating on fire, and… nothing.

"Worthless wand," I complained, putting it back into my pocket. Still full from eating so much food and getting rather sleepy, I considered going without a fire. Then a howl made my hair stand on end and I groaned. "Annoying werewolves." The reason I chose to sleep in the woods instead of out in the open was obvious; werewolves were less of a nuisance than ghosts.

The deciding factor was that the wind was beginning to sound a lot like whispers. I searched my satchel and finally found my pair of snapping rocks and my flame-proof dragon-hide gloves. When I smacked the snapping rocks together, sparks rained from them into the sticks and dried weeds. With some gentle nudging and soft blowing, I got a small fire going.

I was used to sleeping outside at night, but there was something very different about this night and it made my skin crawl. The whispering in the wind was growing more conspicuous, yet I couldn't understand the words.

Right before I fell asleep, I realized what was making me so edgy; there was no wind.

*　　*　　*

I dreamed of opening the chest, unleashing a powerful monster the likes of which Akadema has never seen, defeating Magnus, and finally being known as a sorcerer worthy of the Dracre name. I would just have to make sure the monster didn't hurt anyone. I wanted to cause trouble, not hurt people.

The sound of a very close howl woke me, but I wasn't worried. My dream had given me an idea. I pulled the box out of my bag and hesitated when I heard the whispers again. Whatever it was inside the box was what I was hearing. Assuming it was some trick in order to frighten me away from it, I pulled the wand out of my pocket and waved it at the chest. *Reveal your secrets.*

Instead of the chest opening, the inscription changed so that I could read it.

> *Every choice creates ripples like a stone dropped into a pond. The ripples of many choices merge, alter, and reflect off each other and the bank in unpredictable ways. The greater the choice, the larger the ripples and the more unpredictable the consequences.*

As soon as I read it, the box flew out of my hands, the lid opened with a creak, and light spilled out that was so bright I had to cover my eyes. The whispering became louder until it was an unintelligible hissing. It wasn't out loud, though; it was in my mind. When I heard the lid close and looked at it, my jaw dropped. There was a big wolf with white, grey, black, and auburn fur sitting in front of me.

"What...?" I tried to scramble back only to hit the tree I had fallen asleep under. The wolf snarled. "Please don't eat me!" I said as I put my arms over my face. I had dropped my wand when I first saw the wolf.

The whispering softened suddenly before forming into words. "*I am not going to eat you.*" The voice was strange, masculine, oddly weightless, and nothing like the whispers I heard before.

I looked at the animal in shock; it wasn't a werewolf, skinwalker, or spirit. Actual wolves were rarer than dragons. "Did you just talk?"

His eyes widened. "*You can hear me?*" The wolf's mouth didn't move, yet I heard him very clearly in my mind. When I didn't answer him, he studied the small chest at his feet, obviously reading the inscription. "*I see. You must have said the incantation and used very powerful magic to free me.*"

I hadn't said the inscription aloud and I didn't have very powerful magic. "So you came from the box? I was told the box held an extremely powerful creature."

"*That was correct, except that this is no mere box. The syrus is an ancient device that can contain even the most powerful magic.*"

"Who are you?"

"*My name is Merlin. I am… or rather, I was a wizard. Unfortunately, I loved the wrong person and was blinded to an enemy I should have been able to defeat easily. Instead, I was turned into this and trapped in the syrus.*"

"So, you're a wizard?"

"*That is what I said.*"

"Well, I'm a sorcerer, so we're enemies."

"*A sorcerer? We must be on Caldaca.*"

"We're in Akadema," I corrected him.

He rolled his wolf eyes. "*Akadema is an island. Caldaca is the name of your world. I traveled to many worlds, and only Caldaca is so divided in magic to differentiate between wizards and sorcerers. I was under the impression that sorcerers did not have blond hair on this world.*"

I grimaced. "Yes, I know. I'm really weird. That's why I'm out here; I'm on a quest to prove that I'm a powerful and malevolent sorcerer."

"*You* want *to be malicious? Do you like hurting people or are you just trying to gain riches?*"

"I don't want to hurt anyone. It's just that my family is known for being sorcerers and they're all ashamed of me. I'm going to defeat the great wizard, Magnus. The problem is that I'm very bad at being a sorcerer. Whenever I try to cause trouble, my spell messes up."

"*Your magic reflects who you are inside.*" He was silent for a moment. "*Nevertheless, I think we can help each other. In this cursed form, I cannot do magic. It occurs to me that this great wizard can break the curse, but getting to him alone will be difficult and communicating my needs will be even more challenging. I propose a deal.*"

"I don't work with wizards," I said.

"*On my world, there is no distinction between wizards and sorcerers, as I have never met a wizard who is entirely and inherently good. I have, however, met many vicious villains on my travels. If you assist me in finding this wizard and convincing him to turn me back into a man, I will teach you how to be the most malevolent, successful sorcerer in all of the lands.*"

# CHAPTER 2

Obviously, I accepted Merlin's offer. First of all, Merlin was experienced in magic. Although he was a wizard, he did say that wizards were not all good on his world. Besides, I could learn from him even if it was how to counteract wizardry. Second, Merlin was a wolf; there were few monsters I had to worry about with him next to me. And third, I had no idea how to find Magnus, let alone defeat him.

*"Before I begin teaching you, I need to eat,"* Merlin said.

Excited to be useful for once, I picked up my wand and pulled my last lump of clay out of the bag. "What is it you want?" I asked.

*"Meat, obviously."*

My excitement was doused. "Oh… well… meat isn't very good for you. Are you sure you wouldn't like---"

*"I am a wolf, young sorcerer."*

"My name is Ayden Dracre."

His eyes widened. "*Interesting. You are not by chance related to Ilvera Dracre, are you?*"

"That's my mother. You know her?"

"*I might have… heard of her. If she is your mother, then… oh, yes. Caldaca has a matriarchal society.*"

"I read that it used to be otherwise, but then sorceresses and witches rebelled and created a widespread curse so that all the women of the land could only have daughters. When the first generation of daughters reached the age where they had to fight each other for the few men left, the curse was broken. My father said it cut our population in half and set us back by hundreds of years, giving magic a chance to shape the world. My mother said men were insufferable and didn't deserve to rule anyway. If I got married, I would keep my name, but my children would have my wife's family name."

"*I applaud your knowledge of your world's history. Anyway, young sorcerer, if you would be so kind as to conjure my meal, we can begin our excursion.*"

"Alright." I set the clay on the nearby high root, closed my eyes, and waved my wand. *Please give me meat. Please don't embarrass me. Change into meat.*

"*Hmm,*" Merlin said thoughtfully.

I opened my eyes and groaned. A green apple and three stalks of broccoli were in the place of the magic clay. "I told you I'm a bad sorcerer. I can't even conjure any food other than this."

He studied the food thoughtfully. I studied him thoughtfully. "*I see your predicament,*" he finally said. "*Did you make your wand, buy it, or inherit it?*"

I noticed he didn't ask if I had stolen it. My brothers stole their wands from the best-known wand-maker in all of Akadema, but I could never do that to the poor old man who made his living by providing high-quality, intricately carved tools of magic. "I made it." I explained exactly how I tried to make it and how it transformed the first time I used it.

"*I see,*" Merlin said. "*I cannot understand how anyone could use a wand they bought. Your wand is created with* your *magic and uses* your *magic. Conjuring meat is the same as hunting; it requires a sacrifice of life. The magic inside you is incapable of that, so your wand is incapable of that.*"

I clenched my teeth to keep my mouth shut until I could keep the whining out of my voice. "There is no wizard in my entire family, so I can't possibly have light magic!"

He sighed in my mind. "*I know that occultism on Caldaca is unique, but you seem to misunderstand the foundation of magic. I see that I have much to teach you before you can face Magnus.*"

"If you want Magnus's help, why are you helping me knowing I want to defeat him?"

"*I have my ways, young sorcerer.*" He then nodded to the apple and broccoli. "*Eat while you can and I will hunt for myself.*" He disappeared into the darkness of the forest without another word.

I grimaced and scooped the apple and broccoli into my satchel for later, along with the magic box.

\* \* \*

Soon, the sun peeked over the horizon and Merlin returned. Light streamed through the gaps in the leaves of the trees above and glowed softly against his multi-colored fur. As if he realized how the light accentuated his arrival, he posed for a moment.

"What's the first step in making me a better sorcerer?" I asked.

He sat on his haunches. "*Are you trained in fighting?*" he asked.

I shook my head. "I'm very good at running away and hiding from my brothers."

He tilted his head a little bit as he considered this. "*Very well. To defeat the wizard, you will need to know enough magic to defend yourself and to fight, as well as some powerful weapons and some minions.*"

"Weapons? Like swords?" I asked, hoping I never had to tell him that I turned a bunch of swords into flowers.

"*No. You are not ready for that. I am referring to magical weapons. Your wand is an instrument of your magic that will be incapable of doing anything malevolent unless your soul itself is cruel. Therefore, you will need tools that have their own essence.*"

"We can go to the wand-maker." I pulled the jewelry out of my bag. "I have something we can sell to buy a new wand."

The wolf looked at the jewelry and sighed heavily. "*You understand what being cruel and devious is, right?*"

I frowned. "Right. I'm supposed to steal. But do we have to steal every time? Lorthton is a kind man who doesn't make a lot of money."

"*I will not force your hand; I will only tell you what you must do if you want to be a malicious sorcerer. I personally think you would make a better wizard.*"

I glared at him. "Don't call me a wizard."

"*As you wish. What is it you plan to do as a sorcerer?*"

"Well, I want to be scary and have lots of gold and women and make my brothers afraid of me and… you know… sorcerer stuff. Hey, maybe I could just steal from rich people. That's bad, and I could just say that everyone else doesn't have enough to interest me. If I get too much, maybe I can give some of it to---"

"*Stop right there*," Merlin interrupted. "*I can live with myself after shaping you into the most powerful sorcerer this world has ever seen because that is the way of the land here. I will not, however, bring about the next Robin of Loxely. Finish that thought and I will rescind my offer to assist you.*"

I slipped the loot back into my bag as I made a mental reminder to never mention it again. Apparently, wolves despised charity more than sorcerers did. "Okay."

Merlin decided we needed a place to practice my magic where I didn't have to worry about people getting hurt. He then said that he knew where we could go, but wasn't in the mood to tell me where, so we got back to the dirt road and started the journey to *somewhere*. It seemed like he forgot about me getting a new wand, which I was secretly glad for.

That was until I found out what he had in mind.

\*     \*     \*

Most of the day was spent in silence. I wanted to know about Merlin's world, but he wasn't in a talkative mood. I hoped it was because he had just escaped from the syrus and not because this was as friendly as he got.

"What was it like in the syrus?"

"*Like I was asleep*," he said easily.

"How long were you in there?"

*"There is no way to be sure until I return to a world that keeps an accurate calendar system. It does make world-travel difficult."*

"So you're saying you don't know?"

*"Yes, that is what I am saying."*

"How many times have you been to Akadema?"

*"While I have not been to this particular area before, I have been to this world twice. Of course, twice was quite enough. I find the fact that nearly everyone on your world has magic of one form or another tedious. Necessary for your way of life, yes, but tedious all the same."*

Although it really sounded like he was insulting everyone on this world, he didn't seem to realize he was doing it. "What's wrong with magic? You're a wizard."

*"Yes, well, that is quite different here. If you fall ill, you go to a mage. If you get pregnant, you go to a seer to find out what gender the child is. If you want to speak to long dead loved ones, you go to a necromancer."*

"Actually, if I became pregnant, I wouldn't be going to a seer. I don't know about your world, but men don't get pregnant here."

He gave me a look that simultaneously irritated and confused me, as if he was judging me and wasn't terribly impressed. At that point, I decided not to talk any more.

\*     \*     \*

The sun was low in the sky when the path abruptly ended at the gates of a massive, old, rundown mansion.

A massive mansion which hadn't been there a moment before.

I looked behind us, then back at the mansion, then behind us again. It was not something I could have missed; it was massive.

"*The manor has an illusionary ward over it,*" Merlin explained. "*Until you come upon it, you cannot see the mansion. Fear not; this fort belongs to an old friend of mine.*"

"You have friends?" I asked, earning quite the blood-chilling glare in return. He didn't answer and instead motioned for me to go through the gate. I did, but not without the appropriate amount of complaining and begging that we run as fast as we could in any direction that was away from the mansion.

The gate was old and opened easily, since it didn't have a lock. Merlin's friend probably thought he would never have a problem with bandits on account of the mansion being so creepy that any sane man would run as fast as he could in any direction that was away from the mansion... like we should have been doing.

A cracked stone walkway, overcome with weeds, led to a very grand porch. Thorny vines tried to wrap around my ankles as we made our way to our certain and painful deaths. "Merlin, your friend isn't a cannibal, is he?"

Merlin frowned as thoughtfully as a wolf could. "*Not the last time I saw him.*"

I opened my mouth to ask why that didn't reassure me, thought better of it, and shut my mouth. We reached the porch, which was also cracked and overgrown. When Merlin looked at me impatiently, I reached for the brass knocker on the solid, huge, and faded wooden door. The sound echoed loudly. Slowly, the door opened on its own. "I am not going in there."

"*Suit yourself. Stay outside with the rabbits.*"

"Rabbits?"

"*Of course. What else would a powerful magician use to guard his estate?*"

I shuddered at the thought of being attacked by a vicious rodent with sharp teeth and claws before stepping into the dark interior. The door slammed shut behind me and the fireplace lit itself.

The room was grand, with a high ceiling and dark colors. Bookshelves lined two of the walls, there were two chairs in front of the fireplace, and a large painting of a black dragon hung over the fireplace. On the wall to my left were two doors. On the right was a staircase that led to a balcony.

"Where is your friend?" I asked, turning to Merlin. Then I jumped back with something between a squeak and a feminine shriek, because it wasn't Merlin who stood right behind me.

The man was a head or so taller than me with long, black hair, a trimmed goatee, and stone gray eyes. He wore a black robe with a silver crow clasp at the nape. None of this was what made me shout. Instead, what made my skin try to crawl off and hide under one of the chairs was the fact that the stranger was not completely corporeal.

"You're a…" My voice cracked.

The man narrowed his eyes. "I am Vactarus Firesword!" He held out his hands in a grand gesture and a deep blue glow formed above his palms, which illuminated his face.

"You're a…" My voice cracked again.

"I am the most powerful magician to ever become stranded on Caldaca." The blue glow formed into twin orbs.

"You're a…" My voice cracked for a third time.

"I am the master of this castle." The twin spheres of light suddenly burst into blue fire.

"You're a…"

"*Ayden!*" Merlin admonished.

"Ghost!" I finally got out.

The flames died and the magician crossed his arms and glared at me. "Yes, I'm a ghost. Do you have a problem with that?" His tone told me in no uncertain terms that there was only one answer that wouldn't result in my immediate death.

"Um… no. I'm a sorcerer, so, you know… I see g-ghosts all the time," I lied. Merlin sighed in my mind. "I'm Ayden. If you're a magician, where is your hat?"

"It was stolen by Magnus, the wizard."

"He killed you and took your power?!" I asked, horrified.

The ghost magician pursed his lips and looked at the fire. "Well, no. I tripped over one of my rabbits and fell down the stairs. Magnus took my hat before I learned to control my new ghost powers. Now I can never leave my home, so I cannot get it back."

"Oh, sorry for your loss," I said. Merlin made a sound of disapproval. "I mean… that's not my problem because I'm a sorcerer and I have no sympathy."

"*A sorcerer knows how to choose enemies and allies. Vactarus is a very powerful magician and although magicians only use illusionary magic here, he was once a world traveler and has therefore attained many artifacts you can use as a sorcerer. You are not yet strong enough to steal from someone like Vactarus, but you have a common enemy.*"

"So I should make an alliance with him?" I asked.

"Who are you talking to?" Vactarus asked.

"Merlin. He's the wolf and he can talk to me." The ghost studied Merlin carefully. Merlin sat on his haunches and smirked. I shuddered.

"I knew a wizard named Merlin once. He stole a cushy job I wanted. We dueled and when I won, he was supposed to buy the drinks. Instead, he ran off and left me with the bill."

"*He did not win the duel*," Merlin argued.

"I really don't care," I told the wolf. Vactarus scowled, thinking I was talking to him. "I mean… tell me about it later. I'm going to defeat Magnus and prove myself to be a master sorcerer. If you would be willing to provide me with something I can use to fight him, I'll bring your hat back to you."

"You?" He studied me and obviously found me lacking. "You have no chance of defeating Magnus." Merlin growled at him and he scoffed. "What are you going to do, wolf, bite me?" In response, Merlin went over to one of the chairs and sunk his teeth in to the leather cushion. "No!" the ghost shrieked in utter horror. "Not my custom relaxed leather! It took fifteen virgin maidens to make leather so supple and smooth that also matched my silk curtains!"

Merlin let go of the cushion and glared at the ghost again. "So, you'll help me?" I asked.

The ghost's shoulders slumped. "Your wolf is as uncouth as the wizard I knew who had the same name."

"*I am not uncouth*," Merlin assured me.

"He's not my wolf," I assured Vactarus.

"In the basement of my manor is a secret room full of riches I attained from many different worlds. You may have *one* artifact, only one, and you cannot change your mind later. You can also use the field behind my house and my ritual room to practice your attack. In exchange, you will bring back my hat."

I glanced at Merlin and he nodded. "Deal."

"Then I will return shortly." He vanished.

I grinned widely. "Yay! I got my first accomplice! Or are you my accomplice?"

Merlin just sighed. I didn't care; I was ecstatic to be getting a real magical weapon. A moment later, a young girl appeared right in front of me. This time, I refused to scream. Instead, I mustered every ounce of manliness I could... and squeaked quietly.

Because the young girl was also a ghost.

Her hair was blond and pulled up in pigtails, her blue eyes were huge and doll-like, and her pink cheeks were emphasized by her pale skin. The blue dress she wore was rough on the edges and dirty. She smiled at me. "My name is Kisha."

Vactarus appeared beside her and I squeaked again, less quietly. "Kisha, my daughter, will show you to the vault."

Kisha blushed, smiled shyly at me, and played with the hem of her dress. I squeaked louder until Merlin frowned at me worriedly. That was quite a sight to see, but Merlin seemed to have mastered wolf expressions.

Kisha waved her hand and started towards one of the doors. "Follow me." Merlin and I did.

I opened the door, which revealed a dark hallway. "So... how long have you been... Vactarus's daughter?" I asked, using my natural talent to make everyone in the room extremely uncomfortable.

She laughed. "I'm not really Vactarus's daughter. I was already a ghost here when he took control over the manor. When he died, he sort of adopted me." She walked through another door.

I heard a soft click as the latch released before the door swung open. Merlin and I entered cautiously, immediately having to step down some old, crumbling, stone steps. We followed the steps down until we reached the bottom. I pulled out my wand and let energy flow through me. Since I was very against being trapped in the dark, my magic instinctively knew what to do. The tip of the wand lit up with bright white light that chased away the darkness.

"*No white magic to see here,*" Merlin muttered sarcastically.

In front of us was a stone wall with magic sigils on it. Behind us were only the steps we had descended. "What do we do?" I asked. Kisha was gone and there wasn't another door.

"*Unlock the entrance the same way you did with the syrus.*"

I waved my wand at the wall with the sigils on it. *Reveal your secrets*. Nothing happened. I tried again. *Please open*. Again, nothing happened.

"*These sigils are not weak, but this door can be opened. You have to really want this.*"

I glared at the wall and thrust my wand towards it like I was going to stab it. "Open!" I demanded out loud.

Suddenly, a vertical crack formed in the middle of the wall and grew larger. It was a very straight crack, so I knew it was intentional. I was very glad I wasn't bringing the manor down on top of us. Once was enough for me.

More cracks split the wall until they formed blocks instead of a solid mass. Then, the blocks rearranged themselves to shape a doorway to another secret room. I held my wand out to see inside, since the tip was still glowing. Inside was a larger room, piled high with treasure chests, weapons, and magical items.

"*Very good,*" Merlin said. "*Now, pick out something that feels right to you.*"

"What if I pick out something that only does light magic?"

"*There is nothing associated with white magic in this room.*"

Trusting him, I got to work scouting out the magical items. There were crystal balls, staffs, talismans, rings, etc… I opened a chest and promptly jumped on a nearby table, only to sigh with relief when I saw that it was merely a mummy. At the angle it was stuffed in the chest, it had looked like a large doll. "I don't know what this stuff does."

"*Listen for what speaks to you.*"

I opened my mouth to argue, only to trip and hit the floor with a harsh grunt. Instinctively, I reached for the staff I had tripped over. Two things happened when my fingers wrapped around the wooden rod: I felt an electrical tingle shoot from the staff, through me, and into my wand; and clouds formed above us. It began raining inside.

# CHAPTER 3

Merlin glared at me, so I let go of the staff. Unfortunately, doing so didn't make the rain stop. "Well, this is sorcery, right?" I asked.

The clouds lit up as lightning started to form.

So I grabbed the staff and did what any reasonable person would have done in my situation; I ran like my butt was on fire. I tripped over a chest and ended up rolling the rest of the way out of the room. Merlin leapt out just as the room lit brightly. The blocks rearranged themselves again until it was a wall once more and then the cracks resealed.

I flicked my wand until the end started glowing again. Merlin was still glaring at me. "I didn't mean to do it." He turned and pranced up the steps. His tail was smoking.

*    *    *

Vactarus, Kisha, Merlin, and I sat at the kitchen table in an awkward silence. When we had emerged from the secret room with my new staff, the ghostly hosts insisted we have dinner. Of course, Vactarus and Kisha neither ate nor cooked, so they were sitting and watching us. The fact that the table was covered in dust and set with old dishes didn't seem to bother them. Merlin, who was precariously balanced on the chair, had hunted a rabbit to eat right in front of me. I was eating… an apple and broccoli.

Somehow, I knew if I asked Merlin to share, he would tell me to hunt down my own rabbit because that was what a sorcerer would do. That, or conjure one. I peeked at the sharp claws of the dark black rabbit carcass, shuddered, and ate my broccoli. I didn't want to touch one of them let alone eat one.

The staff, which was propped up against the chair to my right, rattled slightly, as if to get my attention. I reached for it cautiously, and as soon as I touched it, energy shot through me and into the apple in my hand, which suddenly changed into the drumstick of some large bird. *I really am a sorcerer!* "Look!" I said, letting the staff go and waving the meat in front of Merlin's face.

He sniffed it and frowned deeply. "*Tofu?*"

"What's tofu?" I asked. I didn't let his hesitation dampen my excitement. I finally conjured meat and all it took was getting a new magic tool.

"*Tofu is… a very good source of protein. You did a good job,*" he said, sounding more hesitant than anything else.

That confirmation ramped up my excitement another notch and I bit into the meat. It was hot and juicy, but as I chewed, it turned cold. I chewed a little more. And then chewed some more. "Is it supposed to be so…?" I trailed off, unable to come up with a word to adequately describe the elastic flavor or bland texture.

"*Yes, it is*," Merlin assured me. "*We should find out more about that staff before anything dangerous happens.*"

Having grown up with six older brothers, I was no stranger to danger. "What can you tell me about this staff?" I asked Vactarus, picking it up to study closer. The wood was twisted, smooth, and dark with gold-painted sigils carved into it. They weren't anything I recognized from my family's grimoires, but they were definitely black-magic in nature. At the top of the staff was a large, crudely-cut, blood-red, clear stone.

The ghost leered at it. "Oh, it has quite the story. I first came across it on a land that only had women. They got the idea to use it to conjure men to keep them warm and safe in the cold winter nights. I, of course, felt it was my duty to take one for the team, so to speak. I showed them all kinds of fun. In fact, half of them lost their---"

"Please don't finish that sentence," I interrupted. Energy shot from the staff into Vactarus. Unlike my usual magic, which was sparkly, light, and bounced around freely, this was dark and twisted, like a thorny vine, and it went straight for its mark. To my shock, the magic struck the ghost and his mouth snapped shut. No matter how hard he tried to open it, his lips wouldn't part.

"Wow. I have never been able to make him stop talking," Kisha said with awe.

I set the staff down on the dusty table and wiped my hands on my pants. "Sorry, I didn't mean to---"

Merlin made a sound of disapproval.

"I mean… I'm not sorry because I'm a sorcerer and I have no sympathy." I picked up the staff carefully and aimed it at the magician. Kisha and Merlin both ducked under the table, Merlin by diving gracefully and Kisha… by phasing right through the table. "Be able to talk again," I said.

Nothing happened.

I repeated the command while waving the staff dramatically.

Nothing happened again.

Well, something happened. I shrieked and jumped out of my skin when I felt Kisha's ghostly hand gently caress the inside of my thigh. "Merlin, what do I do?!" I asked, forcefully stopping myself from crawling onto the table.

Kisha patted my knee and backed off. "Sorry, handsome, I dropped my fork."

"You weren't eating anything!"

"I was planning on eating something, but Vac wanted to join us for dinner."

"Merlin!" I squeaked.

The wolf sighed in my head. "*Use your wand.*" Quickly following his advice, I set the staff down, pulled out my wand, and aimed it at Kisha. "*On Vactarus,*" Merlin said.

I grunted and aimed it at the magician. "You can talk," I said.

A sunny yellow ball of energy popped out of the tip of my wand, bounced off the table, and hit Vactarus. His mouth opened easily. He snapped it shut, obviously afraid that I would curse him again. Merlin and Kisha returned to their chairs. I sat back down in my seat, picked up my tofu bird, and continued eating. It was foul.

"So, about the staff," I prompted.

Vactarus licked his lips nervously, which was an odd habit for a ghost. "The women gave it to me in exchange for my attention, but I sold it on the next world I came to, which only made sense; it was rubbish at the time. Then, about a year later and ten worlds away, I met a lovely young woman whose family owned a winery. We spent many days lounging in---"

"Get on with it," I said.

"Oh, yes. Anyway, we married and some old lady gave it to me at the wedding. I knew it was the same staff because an item like that cannot be forgotten. It was different, though. There was power in it that was not there when I first saw it. Someone had used it to do very powerful, very dark magic, and that left a stain in the wood and the crystal."

"The crystal?" I asked, looking at the stone on the top. Although it was shaped like a crystal, I had only ever seen black ones used by sorcerers and white ones used by wizards. I had no idea they came in colors.

"Yes, it is a crystal. Surprising, I know; it looks like a massive ruby. It was white when I first saw it, and it only had strands of red when I attained it at my wedding. Nevertheless, my beloved and I were not meant to be. Within a fortnight, she realized she could not tame my need for adventure and danger, so she asked me to leave. Unfortunately, the girl she caught me talking to— which was absolutely not my fault. I was seduced and had no idea her intention was to strip my---"

"Get on with it," I said.

"Oh, yes. I sold it again, since it was the only thing I had been able to grab. Then, about three years later, I saw it in the keep of a most malevolent wizard. The crystal was pure red at this point, and produced an essence as if it was self-aware."

I glanced worriedly at the staff, half afraid it would randomly start blasting curses at us. "So you got it from him?"

"Of course not. I ran away. I had far too much to live for to risk myself for something I neither wanted nor needed. It was about two years later that I found it while hunting for the well-guarded treasure of a dragon. This is the first time I have ever seen the blasted thing ever work for anyone."

"Really? Maybe it likes me." I had never been liked by an inanimate object before. I took another bite of my meat and was certain the texture was actually getting slimier.

"I'm confused," Vactarus said, flinching when I looked at him. "You said you were a sorcerer, yet you don't act like any sorcerer I know. Furthermore, why do you have blond hair?"

*"Tell him it was a disguise spell gone wrong,"* Merlin advised.

I did, which seemed to placate the ghost. I wished I could speak in Merlin's mind like he could in mine. I also wished Kisha would stop batting her eyelashes at me. The staff rattled, but I ignored it.

I was able to eat about half of the bird before I couldn't bring myself to stick another bite of the gelatinous meat in my mouth. Kisha then showed us to a couple of rooms. Along the way, I noticed an inconsistency with the mansion. Several of the paintings were clean of dust and others weren't. There were books and tea cups left out on tables, but nothing rotten. If I had to make a guess, I would say the place was set up to look abandoned.

My bed, though covered in dust, was easily five times the size of mine at home and infinitely softer than the cold dirt. The dark walls were crumbling and the grimy window was covered in cobwebs. The hardwood floor could have used a good sweeping… or scrubbing. I stepped around the large, dried puddle of blood. Dried blood didn't bother me; my mother used blood all the time in her potions. Other than the bed, the sparse furniture consisted of a small table beside the bed with two lit candles and a chest across from it. Surprisingly, the chest contained clean, yet stale clothes that fit me pretty well.

When Kisha left Merlin and me alone without hesitation, I was relieved. I set my wand on the table and leaned my staff against the wall next to it. "Can you teach me to talk in your head like you can mine?" I asked.

He sat. *"You have the skill already, yet you do not know how to use it. I picked it up naturally because it was my only means of communication. You released me from the syrus, and in doing so, you bound us. What all that entails exactly, I do not yet know. All I know is that I am unable to use magic and I have much to teach you."*

"Do you always talk so formally?"

*"Yes. Yes, I do."*

I sat on the bed. "Can you show me a spell to make my hair black?"

*"I am rather surprised your mother never did it."*

"She's done it before, but it always changes back when I do magic."

*"I see. The reason for this is your magic itself. Magic here is not any more limited than it is on other worlds, yet magic users are. It is only reasonable, for magic users could easily destroy this world if not kept in check. In fact, one of the worlds I traveled to had a violent*

*hate for all things supernatural. Their cities were quite fascinating in a technological standpoint, as they were moments away from technological singularity, which was the reason for my premature departure. Yet another world I traveled to was so technologically repressed that the residents of a small village tried to burn me when they saw my watch."*

"Um…" I agreed wisely.

*"But I digress. Your natural appearance is influenced by your magic because that is the nature of this world. This is so that when you encounter strangers, they have an idea what kind of person you are. On this world, untrustworthy people look untrustworthy. Therefore, only* you *can change your appearance and you can only do that by changing who you are. In the meantime, you can simulate such an appearance using illusionary magic."*

"But that means I need a magician."

*"Quite right. Unfortunately, I did not expect Vac to be dead when I thought of him. You will have to live with your blond hair for a while longer."*

To be perfectly honest, I didn't mind my hair color except that it was another reason for my brothers to tease me. "Tell me about the world you're from."

*"I have traveled to many worlds."*

"I know, but where were you born? What was it like growing up? Were your parents wizards? Were they proud of you?"

He sighed. *"I was born on an archaic world with too many superstitions and traditions. I never knew my father, but my mother had no shortage of tales to spin. I was told my power was noticeable from birth and my mother would never admit to bedding a man out of wedlock, so it was said that my father was a demon. You can imagine the rumors I had to suffer through. When I was nine, I discovered how to travel to different worlds."*

"I bet that was scary."

"*It was rather confusing at first. It began with astral projection.*"

"With what?"

"*I traveled to other worlds in my mind, which I learned by accident. Once I met some others with the same abilities, I practiced and studied the magic necessary to travel the worlds. One day, I told my mother that I would find a better place to live and come back for her. I traveled to so many worlds that they began to blend together. It was amazing and beautiful and lonely. I found a world I knew my mother would be happy on. It was frightfully boring, but then, so was my mother. I was too late, though. I returned to the home I was born in to find that it had been passed on to another family. She had died alone, still waiting for me to come back.*"

"She didn't have any other children?"

He shook his head. "*I never knew why for sure, but I believe she was hoping for my father to return. I spent many years after that traveling from world to world. When I was very lonely, I would settle down somewhere for a few years, but eventually something out there would call to me and I would take off again. I saw so many incredible things, so much history unfolding in front of my very eyes... yet there was no one to share it with. The majesty of the universe was not meant to keep secret.*"

"Why didn't you take an apprentice or something?"

"*I did eventually. I took a number of them over my many years instead of having children. In the end, though, they would leave to experience their own adventures. Some of them fell in love, some of them broke down under the weight of what they saw, and some of them just moved on. I also became an adviser to non-wizards. Unfortunately, too often, people did not really believe in my magic.*"

"How old are you?"

"*I never bothered to figure that out.*"

I really didn't think I could hear any more that night. It never occurred to me that being stuck in wolf form was the least of the wizard's problems. "How did you end up cursed? I know you said that you loved the wrong woman and was blinded to your enemy, but how?"

*"That is a story for another night."*

I figured as much. "How did you end up on this world? You didn't know what world this was until I said I was a sorcerer."

*"Yes, I was on a different world; one where I was quite the legend. If anything, I was more feared there than Magnus is here. How I came to be here, I have no idea. Someone must have stolen the syrus and brought it here. I am still unsure how you read the inscription."*

"I don't know. I just waved my wand and told the box to open. The inscription became readable, I read it, and the syrus opened. I'm pretty tired."

*"Then I will leave you for tonight. In the morning, you will begin practicing with your new staff."* He turned and left.

After shaking the blanket to rid it of the dust, I sat back down and studied my new staff. Energy tingled under my skin as it adapted to the power. It was almost as if the staff and my magic were getting to know each other.

Worried that I was going to accidentally do magic, I set it back down and settled under the covers. A moment later, I turned… and squeaked. Then I fell out of bed with a pained grunt. "What are you doing?!" I asked Kisha, who was lying on the bed. I had never had a bed large enough to share with a girl, and I definitely didn't want a young ghost to be the first one I shared it with.

She smiled shyly. "I just wanted to make sure you are settled in and have everything you need." She twirled a lock of blond hair around her index finger. "I thought your wolf would never leave."

"Actually, I think I forgot to ask him a question. I should go find him." I turned to the door, only for her to suddenly appear in front of it. *Gods*. "Or not. I'm really tired and I think I should go to bed." Her smile fell and I felt bad. Not bad enough to invite her to stay, but still pretty bad.

"Oh. Okay," she said. "I guess I'll see you tomorrow." With that, she vanished.

# CHAPTER 4

I woke up to the scent of eggs and potatoes, and my stomach growled. Beside my bed was a plate with a generous portion of eggs along with seasoned potato cuts mixed with cheese and onion. I spared a moment to wonder who had prepared the meal before I devoured it like I was starving.

When I was finished, I dressed, grabbed my wand and staff, and left to explore the mansion. All of the bedrooms were on the second floor. Right before I reached the staircase, I happened to glance into a room to my left and stopped. It was a huge library, which I couldn't resist. I closed myself in the room and studied the books. Most were ancient grimoires on magic, yet others were about mythology or grand quests.

It was too warm for me to light the fire, so I pulled a few books down and sat on the window seat to read.

\*　　\*　　\*

"*This is not where I expected to find you, young sorcerer,*" Merlin said, pulling me back to reality. I glanced out the window and realized it was far past morning. Merlin sat in the center of the room, looking almost amused.

"I like books," I said. "Mother only ever let me read about curses and potion ingredients."

"*Who taught you to read?*" he asked.

"My father. He had a lot of older brothers, like me, so he often took pity on me when my mother wasn't around."

"*You are not, by chance, the seventh son of the seventh son, are you?*"

"Yes, I am. Why?"

He hesitated. "*We should discuss that another time. For now, let us begin your training. Pick up the staff, and attack me.*"

"Attack…" I looked around at all the flammable paper. "But the books would get hurt." Merlin gave me a scowl, turned, and walked out. I was very glad he didn't push. Yes, I wanted to be a malevolent sorcerer, but that was no excuse to destroying books. I followed him out of the room, down the stairs, and through a back door.

Behind the mansion was a grassy field. It wasn't lush, green, and trimmed like I had imagined it would be. No, it was more befitting the house; the field had waist-high, brown grass and was speckled with boulders, thorn vines, and abandoned, half-disintegrated battle equipment. "*Is this to your bibliophile satisfaction?*"

"My what?"

"*Never mind. You apparently have more depths than I had originally thought.*"

"Oh," I said, assuming he was insulting me. My brothers ridiculed me for pretty much everything I did, but most of all for my desire to read books. Of course, none of them could read, so they didn't know what they were missing. I felt a little stab of pity for them.

*"Put your wand away and attack me with magic."*

I stuck my wand in my pocket and put both of my hands on the staff in front of me. *Attack*, I thought to the staff. Nothing happened. *Fire*. Still nothing.

*"Any time now,"* Merlin said.

"I'm trying. I'm thinking it really hard."

*"Thinking a command is not the same as feeling it. When you conjure food, you do not* think *food, you* feel *hunger. When you silenced Vactarus last night, you wanted it. To attack someone, you have to* feel *it."*

"But I don't want to attack you." He gave me a thoughtful look. Again, I was astounded by his skill in making expressions with his wolf face.

*"I see. I suppose I have no other choice. Prepare yourself to be offended,"* he said. Before I could say anything, he continued. *"Your blond hair makes you look like my first girlfriend, who was twelve. Your wand looks like a stick of cherry-flavored chocolate. You smell feminine. Your magic is whiter than my teeth."*

"Hey! That's rude! Don't talk about my magic that way."

*"Your mother is a warlock."*

"My mother is not a deceiver with no real magic!" It wasn't the first time someone had called her a trickster, but it was usually the last thing they ever said. Warlocks, who had no magic, were often trying to pass themselves off as sorcerers, so they were despised by all real sorcerers.

*"She is, and you are a wizard."*

I knew he was only trying to rile me up, and he had so much as told me it was coming, but I still felt anger boil in my blood. It was different when my family insulted me; they knew my weaknesses and I knew theirs. We were stuck with each other whether we liked it or not. Merlin didn't know me or my evil mother.

The crystal on the staff started emitting a dim glow, and the knowledge that I was doing something was all the encouragement my anger needed. I thought of what I wanted to strike with, but that only made the glow begin to fade.

It was my mother's words that came to mind, not Merlin's. *"In any battle it is the one who has nothing to lose that wins,"* she had said many times. As always, her words were entirely unhelpful. The crystal faded more.

*"Sorcerers need no reason to be angry, Ayden,"* Merlin said, abandoning his ploy to incite me. *"All magic comes from inside us. Even magical objects were born of the power inside a person. It is pure, manifested desire, for sorcerers and wizards alike. Wizards may desire peace and balance while sorcerers may desire self-gain and raw power, but the more powerful person is the one with a stronger desire. The only way you can beat me is to want a victory more than me. That is why sorcerers find so many reasons to hate and to hold grudges. I have never actually met a happy sorcerer."*

"My mother is happy," I said. Well, at least I thought so. The fact was, nothing was ever good enough for her, even from my oldest brother, who was her favorite. She always smiled a lot, though, and while it was usually a cruel or treacherous grin, I thought it meant that she was happy.

*"Of course she is not. After birthing six suitably obedient pawns, her plans were foiled by the son she had been waiting for all along. I suppose you must be the greatest disappointment to her."*

I started to argue before I realized what he was saying. "What does this have to do with my brothers? You said something about it earlier, too."

*"We can discuss that later. For now, you are in the midst of a lesson, and you have yet to strike me."*

The staff had stopped glowing completely. "I don't want to fight you. I appreciate that you're trying to rile me by insulting me, but I also know it's not true."

He sighed in my head. *"This may be the root of your problem. No sorcerer is so self-aware and unaware at the same time. It is true that I did not mean what I said when I insulted you, but a sorcerer does not care. A sorcerer can turn on anyone for no reason at all."*

"What stops a sorcerer from walking into traps every day?"

*"Nothing on other worlds; they rush into traps quite frequently. Here, however, people value sorcerers as much as wizards for the same reason people do not normally hate sharks. Thus, it does not happen so much. Now, stop stalling and attack me."*

I was stalling, but I wasn't wasting time. First, I tried to make myself angry. Unfortunately, I couldn't think of anything to be angry about. I didn't think it would be wise to point this out. Instead, I focused on the desire to prove that I was not a wizard. I would prove myself by defeating the greatest wizard of the land and then my family would stop ridiculing me at every turn.

The crystal started to glow softly again. *This is it. I can do this. I can use dark magic.* I would have gone on, encouraged by the energy I could feel thrumming in the staff and my own energy that was starting to prickle under my skin, but that was when the ground exploded upward right in front of me.

I shrieked and my magic shot through the staff before I realized that the ground hadn't actually exploded. Instead, it was Vactarus who had popped up. Unfortunately, I couldn't stop the magic once it had left me. Bright red energy struck Vactarus, and his body instantly shrunk and transformed into a little black bat.

"Oh, so cute!" I cooed before I could stop myself. My mother only let us have large, outside bats that could defend the house and warn us when people wandered too close, so the little bat was pretty adorable in my opinion. Unfortunately, my brothers didn't know how to take care of a bat and thus, we never kept one for long.

"Cute?!" Vactarus squeaked, his voice high-pitched. "Turn me back!" He was only able to flap his little wings a few times before he plummeted to the ground.

I held the staff out to Merlin. "Maybe you should do it."

The wolf smirked. "*Actually, I think not. You turned a* ghost *into a ghost* bat. *I am rather impressed.*"

I grinned as well. It wasn't anything as malevolent as what even my nicest brother did on a daily basis, but it was real sorcery. "Sorcerers have minions, right? Can I have an army of bat minions?"

Merlin rolled his eyes. "*Not if you coo at them every time you see them.*"

Vactarus didn't hear Merlin and obviously didn't like being ignored, because he flapped his wings in fury. I resisted making another adoring sound as he was lifted into the air and landed on his head. "Turn me back!" he screeched.

I almost aimed the staff at him, but stopped myself right before doing so. Although breaking curses was not sorcery, it took an understanding of the magic that caused the curse. I didn't understand what I had done, and I definitely wasn't going to be able to undo it with my new staff.

"*You were able to remove the silencing curse last night,*" Merlin reminded me, obviously understanding my hesitation.

"I think removing my own curse should be easy, because I know my magic." Or, at least that was what I told myself. The fact that I could easily break my brothers' curses never failed to anger my mother. It was just easier for me to undo dark magic than to do it.

Also, as often as my brothers cursed me, it was a life-or-death skill. The first one I ever broke was my eldest brother's, because he cursed me to stop breathing whenever I fell asleep. Unfortunately, when I tried to curse him to bleed profusely from every orifice, my magic just made him smell like wild berries instead.

I laid my staff gently on the ground and pulled out my wand. My energy responded readily, as if my wand was a welcomed friend I hadn't seen in a while. I pointed it at the ghost bat and thought, *return to normal.* Magic flashed. It was white for once, as if it didn't have time to be colorful and sparkly and utterly embarrassing. To my great relief, it didn't even do a fluttery dance. It struck Vactarus and he immediately changed back into a man… well… ghost.

He righted himself and glared at me. Since he was a spirit instead of a physical person, I wasn't surprised that his clothes were perfectly unruffled.

"Sorry. You shouldn't sneak up on Dracre sorcerers. We tend to curse first and ask questions later," I said. Merlin raised an eyebrow at me. "At least, everyone else in my family does."

Vactarus's eyes widened dramatically and I realized that I had never told him my family name. "You are a Dracre?!" Before I could answer, understanding filled his eyes. "I see. You resemble Livia quite well."

"Who?" I didn't know a Livia, but I did know I didn't resemble any of my family members.

*"Ask him why he interrupted the lesson,"* Merlin said.

I did, and Vactarus said, "Oh, yes. I just wanted to inform you that there is a seer tournament this afternoon in a village to the north, in case you wanted to see it."

"Yes!" I exclaimed excitedly. I snuck out to see one every time I heard one was near.

*"We have no time for playing around. Are you not in a hurry to get to the wizard before your brothers?"* Merlin asked.

"Well, yes, I am, but my brothers are pampered and won't move quickly. They will probably stop at every village along the way for food, shelter, and women. Besides, maybe we can talk to one of the seers who can help us with either your curse or finding Magnus."

*"Perhaps, but seers are extremely dangerous and often devious."*

"They are? None of the seers that I ever met were devious. We can go?"

He sighed. *"Very well. I reserve the right to place all the blame on you when we end up captured and eaten by trolls."*

I scoffed. "It's not troll season."

\*       \*       \*

We had to leave right then to make it to the tournament. I could hear the crowd before we could see it, but the village was not too far from Vactarus's mansion. When we reached the top of a hill that overlooked the town, I sighed. "Well, it's not the biggest tournament, but I guess that's because of the season."

The village itself was a fair size and surrounded by vast fields of crops. The houses and shops were made of wood, mud, and straw, but cloth tents were crammed between them and around the village in a lively display of color.

Merlin gave me a look. *"There are hundreds of people there to watch other people throw casting stones and stare into crystal balls."*

I gaped at him. "What kind of seer tournaments have you been to? You can get food from all over the world, trade mystical artifacts, and hear your fortune. Of course, the main event is watching the seers try to outclass each other. Their magic gets really chaotic after a while. This is small compared to some of them that I've been to." I was already heading towards the town before he could argue.

Unfortunately, that didn't even slow him down. *"That is another reason that we shouldn't be here. Nothing good ever comes of divination."*

"Of what?" I asked.

*"Never mind."*

By the time we made it down the hill, I was sweating in my thick sorcerer robes and using my sorcerer's staff a little too roughly. Fortunately, I had left my bag and wand at the castle. It felt weird not having them on me, but

Merlin said they detracted from the sorcerer image as much as my hair and eye color.

The tents were so cramped and open to allow air flow that I could see multiple events at once. I knew once the competitions began that the tents would close to cut out the sound. People who were local and recognized my family by the emblem on my robe gave me lots of space. Others spotted Merlin and decided that something on the opposite end of the event was desperately interesting.

Traders traveled the world and were well-respected, but some focused on trading magical items. Since wizards and sorcerers were basically stationary, they were not typically targets of traders. Thus, they focused on the novelty of magic, and there were no better examples of that than the tournaments of seers, shapeshifters, and magicians.

Traders usually followed these tournaments all year, but people had to be careful when buying from them since some were not part of the guild. It was dangerous buying from a private trader, because they could steal something potentially lethal and sell it to someone else without proper instructions. This was particularly worrisome when it came to curses and grimoires.

And they knew how to display their wares. Lightning struck the ground right in front of me, but I ignored it. They could sell enough magic to make anyone feel like a wizard or sorcerer, yet I was only interested in finding something that could help me defeat Magnus.

Still, I couldn't stop myself from pausing at several tents to observe random people hearing about their fame and fortunes, even if it wasn't true. After all, no one paid to hear they were going to die soon or lose all their riches.

The competitions themselves were much bolder. A seer once told a person he was going to die in a horrific and terrible way before the end of the day. He had a heart attack from fear and died.

When I told Merlin, his demeanor soured. He really didn't like seers.

Because there were so many people, I didn't sense that I was being followed until I felt a gentle tug on my sleeve. I turned and jumped back to avoid the sharp horn of a unicorn… again. "What are you doing here?" I asked, realizing as I said it that it was the same unicorn from the other village. The unicorn tossed his head and nickered.

*"He came for you. He must think you need his help,"* Merlin said. *"Would you care to explain what you did to make this unicorn like you so much?"*

"I didn't do anything. Please go away! I don't need any help." The unicorn tossed his head again and pranced away. I continued walking without another word to Merlin.

"Can I interest you in a leash for your wolf?" a trader asked, stopping in front of me so suddenly that I had to brace myself on Merlin. Since Merlin advanced on the man with a vicious snarl on his face, it looked like I was just trying to hold Merlin back.

"Have you ever tried to put a leash on a wolf?" I asked.

With his eyes wide, he looked like he wanted to bolt. "No. I've never even seen a real wolf."

"That's because the people who try to leash wolves are eaten." The words were barely out of my mouth before he vanished into the crowd.

I stopped at an information booth and studied the schedule. There were mostly shows going on, none of which were helpful, and the traders rotated throughout the grounds. I considered looking for some explosive powders, but that stuff had a history of exploding in its owner's pockets. Besides, I definitely didn't think I could *blow* the wizard up.

"What about an invisibility spell?" I asked, turning to Merlin. Only, the wolf wasn't there. "Merlin?" I called, glancing around. When he didn't immediately appear, I turned back to the charts that were nailed all over the walls of the booth. I wasn't terribly worried; Merlin was a wolf with wizard knowledge, so he was certainly safe. Plus, if he wasn't, he could talk in my head. As for me, it wasn't my first time at places like this. Therefore, I wasn't worried.

That was, until I heard two very familiar voices.

I turned and my heart dropped into my stomach. Zeustrum and Bevras were standing so close to me that I could have poked them with my staff. For the moment, they were too busy arguing with each other to see me.

Bevras and Zeus braided their hair the same, wore the same clothes, and carried identical swords. The only way to tell them apart was by the scar Bevras had on his right cheek. They both looked like our father except for their eyes, which were the same burgundy color that all Dracre had, yet neither of them had my father's ability to exert his dominance with a single glare. That was just an excuse for them to use violence instead. Zeustrum had a dangerous mixture of patience and vileness. He devised the most ingenious, sinister plots and could wait years for them to fall into place.

Bevras, on the other hand, jumped headfirst into every fight. It was said that the only reason Bevras was born second was because he fought during the entire event. He tried to challenge our father and that was why he had the scar. Our father humiliated Bevras in scarring him because the twins were always distinguishable afterwards. Zeus never treated his twin the same again.

I acted on instinct; I ran backwards until I hit a solid wall. Then I turned slightly, keeping my eyes on them, and ran backwards again.

My back came up against a tent and since the wall was cloth, I fell against it. Apparently, there was a flap there, because I landed inside the tent. Something hard and pointy broke my fall, but part of the tent collapsed on top of me. I struggled to climb to my feet. Right before I could pick up my staff and decide on a direction to go in, I felt a knife press against my back.

"Explain yourself."

# CHAPTER 5

"I'm just a spectator who stumbled backwards into your tent. I'm sorry and I'll pay for any damages." It was my opinion that the back was the worst place to have a dagger against, but I didn't dare move.

"You don't fool me, sorcerer. Did another seer hire you to sabotage me?" It was a harsh, angry, female voice.

"No, honestly, I don't even know who you are." *If only I could reach my staff.*

I contemplated trying to make a grab for it, and thought better of it. It didn't matter how great or terrible I was in magic when she had a dagger to my back and I didn't have any magical weapons. While I could technically do lesser magic without any tools, I never had much practice. That was more of a wizard thing.

As if it knew my plight, the staff started trembling like it was trying to muster up enough power to rise up. *Come on. You can do it. Please come to me.* The dagger dug harder into my back and my staff went still as panic set in. "Please don't hurt me. I just want to walk out of here alive."

The dagger moved away slightly. "I have never heard a sorcerer beg before." There was a tense silence for a moment before the dagger disappeared altogether. "Ayden?"

I turned and gaped. "Dessa?" The seer was as tall as my mother, but pretty much the opposite of her in every other way. She had long white hair and kind blue eyes. Her face, while symmetrical and pleasant, was soft and pale. Even her lips were unpainted. She wore a simple, white dress with see-through sleeves and silver slippers.

"I thought I told you to stop coming to these events," she said, trying and failing to sound harsh. I easily heard the concern in her warm voice.

Dessa was one of the rare seers who took on apprentices and that was the only reason she went to tournaments. She was a true master of the art, but she didn't fit into the stereotypes. When her eyes turned solid white, I picked up my staff.

"Ayden," she said softly, with even more concern.

I didn't bother speaking back to her because she wasn't actually talking to me. While her sight was active, she was blind and deaf to the mortal realm. She could see my soul, my past and future, but not what I was doing at the time. This was what made her so unique; she could go far deeper into her magic than probably any other seer in the world, but it was dangerous. When she was a child, she had gone into a vision and couldn't close her sight for three years. Unfortunately, although she saw her parents' deaths and knew how to stop them, she couldn't bring herself out in time to warn them.

I took the time to look around. Her tent was very dark, as always, but I didn't see any indication that her apprentice was with her. *Where is he?* Dessa was never supposed to be alone. A lot of people wanted her dead and during her visions was the perfect time to strike.

"You have quite the adventure ahead of you," Dessa said, finally coming out of it.

"I'm going to defeat Magnus, the great wizard, and prove to my family that I'm a real sorcerer."

"Your plans have never gone as you expected."

"But I've never been so willing to work hard before. Mother will kill me if I don't prove myself."

"There is more than one way to skin a cat," she said.

"She's going to skin me?!"

She sighed. "I knew the first time I met you that you were something special. Unfortunately, if I tell you outright what your fate is, you will make the wrong choices. Even my powers are limited. I can see what you are meant to do and the consequences of your choices, but not which choice you will make, because you still have time to change your future. All I can tell you is to be true to your heart and let Merlin guide you. He already knows what you must do and he may be the only one who can help you achieve your potential."

That was actually the clearest information I had ever gotten from Dessa. "And one of these choices leads to Mother skinning me?"

"One of the paths you face will lead to your mother killing you, yes. Trust Merlin and follow your heart."

"Sorcerers don't follow their hearts. We have to be conniving and ambitious at all times."

"Why?"

"Because… reasons. I'll try to listen to Merlin, but I still don't want to hurt anyone. I know I can be ruthless and dangerous like my family without killing people or stealing from people who don't have anything to begin with."

"You give your family too much credit. There is one more thing I can tell you, however. What you seek is in the Island of Light."

"That's where Magnus is? Where is the Island of Light?"

"Find a traveler who knows."

I rolled my eyes. "Seriously? I'm in a hurry. Can't you just use your seer magic and tell me? If my brothers get there first---"

"Magnus's castle is not easy to find. It goes wherever it wants to go. You can walk endlessly in every direction and never find him. Think of it as a journey instead of a destination."

I sensed something approaching me. It was powerful, ancient even, and definitely not my brothers. Being able to sense someone was new to me, yet before I could figure out how I developed this ability, Merlin appeared through the flap. It was him I had sensed, so I figured it was related to hearing his words in my mind.

*"I think I have found a way to disguise your hair temporarily without the use of a magician, which will be unaffected by your magic."* There was a white cloth sack tied around his neck.

"How temporarily?"

I could feel his disapproving frown in my mind. *"Did you run into trouble already?"* he asked, looking pointedly at Dessa.

"Yes, I did. My brothers are out there. This is Dessa. I met her at a seers' tournament a few years back. She's a friend. Dessa, as you know, this is Merlin. He's a wizard, but he's from a world where wizards aren't just good and he's training me to be a sorcerer."

"*You have seer friends?*" Merlin asked, unimpressed.

"Of course. Just because we don't do the same kind of magic doesn't mean we can't help each other. My mother says it's not right, but she might be a little behind the times."

Merlin sighed, which he seemed to be doing more and more as he got to know me. "*I have my work cut out for me.*" He didn't say anything more when he saw Dessa's eyes, as she had gone back into her visions.

It was extremely unsettling, but I felt like it was a little rude to stare. Before I could say anything, it was over. "I know who cursed you and how," Dessa said to Merlin.

The wolf's face became even more serious. "*Ayden, please leave the room.*"

"Why?"

"*This is a private matter and I would rather hear it alone if she has anything of value to tell me.*"

"But she can't hear you speak."

"*Unlike you, young sorcerer, I am able to listen without speaking.*"

"What about my brothers?"

"*Ayden,*" he groaned tiredly.

"Alright, I'm going. It was good to see you again, Dessa." I left, but I didn't stray far. With no idea where my brothers had run off to or if my mother was near as well, I sat down and leaned against a support beam of another tent.

To my horror, I heard another couple of familiar voices an instant before the tent flap opened. My youngest two brothers exited, right next to me. Although Mikron and Thaddeus were not my cruelest siblings, neither of them would hesitate to turn me in.

They were slender, more like our mother than our father, but that was no disadvantage to them. Whereas Thaddeus preferred to fight with magic, Mikron was more similar to Bevras in that he wanted to fight with his hands. Mikron had grown his hair long and braided it like our eldest brothers, but when he angered our mother by messing up a batch of potions, she burned his hair off. It was still pretty short no matter how many hair growth tonics he made. Thaddeus kept his hair short like our father.

I clutched my staff tightly, knowing for sure that if they spotted me before I could curse them, I wouldn't have a chance. Neither of them had a wand out, though. My brain rushed to come up with a curse as magical energy tingled under my skin.

Thaddeus looked right at me… and turned away.

I gaped as they both walked off. After a moment, I looked down at myself, wondering if I had somehow become unrecognizable. I didn't shriek when I saw myself, but only because I didn't see myself.

My hands, arms, feet, legs… everything about me including my staff and clothes, was completely invisible.

I didn't shriek.

I might have squeaked a little.

\*       \*       \*

Merlin emerged soon after, easily following his nose right to me. He tilted his head slightly. "*I take it you saw your brothers again.*"

"It was different brothers. I saw them and wanted to hide or something, but instead... I think my staff turned me invisible, and now I don't know how to turn back."

"*Alright. Because your siblings are near and you are not ready to face them, we will leave the tournament before I help you return to normal.*"

"You can fix this?"

"*Of course. What kind of wizard do you take me for?*"

Maybe it was just his confidence, but his words went a long way in making me feel better. It was more difficult getting through the crowd like this, since people didn't move out of my way. By the time we made it out, people were starting to talk about someone being invisible in the crowd. They assumed I was stealing stuff, because why else would someone become invisible in a seer tournament?

We stopped as soon as we were out of sight of the village. "*How does it feel?*" Merlin asked.

"Scary," I answered. He sighed, so I thought hard to come up with a different answer. "Well, it's cold. My whole body is a little cold and tingly, but numb at the same time. I don't like it."

"*Put your staff down and sit in a comfortable position,*" he said. I leaned it against a boulder. As soon as I let go of it, the staff appeared. "*Now, close your eyes and---*"

"My eyelids are invisible!" I whined too loudly before closing them anyway. "Okay, they're closed."

*"Imagine you are bathing in a lake. Imagine the water is frigid and that is why your body is so cold."* He paused for me to imagine it.

Instead of helping, however, it just made me shiver. It was easy to see it in my mind since I took many such baths in the winter.

*"Good. Now, imagine the sun shining into the water. It does not matter how cold the water or air is, because sunlight can easily warm it. The water warms slowly, almost imperceptibly, but your blood starts warming faster than the water."*

As he said this, I felt the sunlight on me, warming me faster than the water I was imagining. "That's weird."

*"The reason your body is warming so quickly is because the energy inside you is starting to move. It is becoming active. The energy that filled you from the staff, making you invisible, is being forced out and into the cold water. You no longer need it. Do you feel the water warming?"*

"Yes."

*"That is the foreign energy being dispersed. The sun is not important, because your energy is taking over. It knows you are safe and no longer needs to be invisible."*

I directed my focus away from the sunlight as I started feeling too warm. Then, suddenly, I realized I couldn't see through my eyelids. In shock, I opened my eyes and looked down at myself. "It worked!"

Merlin's eyes narrowed. *"Of course it worked. I told you it would. The power inside you is stronger than you know. Understand that most spells and curses are easier to break by gently working them off from their weakest points."*

"So, did you find out how to break your curse?" I asked.

"No." Instead of explaining, he turned and walked away.

\*     \*     \*

On the way back to the mansion, I told him about what the seer said to me. "Do you know where the Island of Light is?"

"*I am not that knowledgeable of Caldaca's geography. If I had my magic, I could find the place, but magic-users here are limited in what they can do. As a wizard of a different world, I can do scrying as well as any seer here can, but I understand why power is limited here.*"

"What is scrying?"

"*Crystal gazing.*"

"So wizards can be seers where you're from?"

"*It is more that wizards are all magic users in one where I come from. We can specialize in something, like necromancy or soothsaying, but the possibilities succeed that of wizards here. Instead of having sorcerers, we have wizards that are capable of being just as conniving and malevolent as sorcerers.*"

I spent the rest of the trip in deep thought. On Merlin's world, I wouldn't be judged for being too nice or for my blond hair. Although my magic would still be the same, people would assume I could do more. Right before we reached the gates of the mansion, I opened my mouth to ask him if we could go to his world.

"*Of course, they also kill wizards where I live.*"

"What?!"

"*Well it is complicated. I have been alone and away from society for so long that I cannot be sure what the laws are anymore.*"

That was the moment I realized world-travel was potentially very dangerous.

Inside, there was a plate of fish, corn, and potato slices ready at the table for me. I sat down while Merlin went rabbit hunting. "Who cooked this?" I asked Vactarus. Just like the night before, he and Kisha sat at the table with nothing to eat. This was obviously an important tradition for them.

"Our housekeeper, of course."

I studied the dust all over the table. "Housekeeper?"

"Yes. We want to make sure the mansion stays in a creepy enough state that it scares away bandits without actually falling apart. Since my hat was taken by Magnus, the illusion over the mansion is ever so slowly disintegrating. Soon, there will be nothing left and anyone can find us."

I figured he wasn't trying to pressure me to hurry up and battle Magnus, but I felt guilty for going to see the tournament anyway.

"When are you going to battle Magnus already?"

Okay, my guilt was completely gone. "When I'm ready. Do you know where the Island of Light is?"

"Not on this world. I know where the *tunnel* of light is, and I'm never going there. I'm afraid I have never seen anything of Caldaca outside of Akadema."

"I need to find someone who knows. I need a way to get there, too. I need a plan."

"You need a minion."

I thought about it. It was definitely something a sorcerer would want, although I didn't think turning Vactarus back into a bat was a good idea. My mother saw her children as her minions. "You're right. Do you think I can buy one somewhere?" I certainly wasn't going to grow my own.

Vactarus gave me an annoyed stare. "*Summon* one," he said, as if I should have thought of that on my own.

I definitely should have thought of that on my own.

Merlin returned then with a dead rabbit in his jaws. Well, I thought it was dead, until it tried to scratch at Merlin's throat with its razor-sharp claws. Merlin shook his head until his prey fell still, and then he hopped up on the chair and set it on the table.

The food in my stomach rebelled. "Merlin, will you teach me to summon a beast to help fight Magnus?" I asked.

"*Do you think you have the mental strength and inner peace to control a beast?*"

"Inner peace? That's a wizard thing."

Once again, I could feel his irritation. "*That is a control thing. You cannot control another creature if you cannot control yourself. How easily you picked up my guidance today showed me that you have the skill; you need only to use it.*"

"Then let's go do it."

"*Patience, young sorcerer; the only thing worse than an angry wolf is a hungry one.*" With that, he started eating his rabbit.

"I think I'll just wait outside." I narrowly escaped without losing my dinner. I also learned that I would rather conjure something than hunt my own food.

For a while, I studied the designs on my wand and staff. My wand was as elegant and wizard-like as always. My staff, however, seemed to be a little different than before. The wood was a little smoother, as if it had been polished. The crystal at the top was also slightly lighter than the deep red it had been before. Of course, it was sunset, so my light was starting to fade.

I thought about what I could do to Magnus with my staff. The three times I had used it, it didn't go as planned. Although my wand only did white magic, it was reliable.

Magnus was the most powerful wizard known, so I knew I couldn't just defeat him with magic. What made my family so famous was my mother's skill in coming up with diabolical plans. I was smarter than my brothers, which only angered my mother more because I was the least ambitious. I didn't want to take over Akadema any more than I wanted to curse people and sell them the anti-curse at a ridiculous price.

It wasn't even that I didn't know what I was doing. The first potion I ever had to make was supposed to make someone's hair fall out. However, I thought the ingredients were gross, and I was very young at the time, so I used different ingredients to make an uncontrollable laughing potion instead.

Defeating Magnus would not be a matter of who had the stronger magic. To prove I was a masterful sorcerer, I would have to set an ingenious trap.

# CHAPTER 6

By the time Merlin arrived, only the two full moons provided light. "*Are you prepared?*" he asked. I nodded. "*Very well. Sit, and focus on the energy inside you. Before you can conjure a creature of great power, you must be able to control it,*" he said.

I didn't like the sound of that. As I turned my focus on my energy, Merlin started sniffing at the ground. "What are you looking for?" He ignored me and began digging something up. I realized what it was an instant before he dropped a carrot in my lap. "No!"

"*Rabbits are minor nuisances as long as you avoid their claws and teeth.*"

That was easier said than done. I didn't even have time to jump up and shout something very unmanly before the high grass started to rustle. The field was entirely to their advantage, because I couldn't see them and they could smell me. One rabbit came close enough that I could see him. He was light brown in color and not the largest I had seen. He wasn't looking at me or advancing on me, which I knew was a trap; he was studying me, deciding if I was worth fighting or not.

When the rabbit made a little hop towards Merlin, the wolf growled. Then, with a final sniff in my direction, the rabbit hopped away.

I sighed. "Maybe I was wrong about rabbits. That was totally---" My words were interrupted by my shrill scream of horror and agony as the rabbit pounced on me from behind and sunk its claws into my back. When I reached for my staff that I had dropped, another rabbit leapt out of the grass and sunk its fangs into my hand. By dropping and rolling, I was able to dislodge the rabbit from my back, but I also lost some precious skin when I tore my arm away from the second rabbit. My wand stabbed me painfully in the side, so I pulled it out and waved it around myself. *Protect.*

The wand answered, but in the most unlikely way; magic shot from the wand into the staff, and then from the staff into me. What came out was a mixture of the sinister red energy of the staff and the elegant white energy of the wand. I felt my skin become cold and tingly again. A third rabbit appeared and bit my hand, but this time, I didn't feel it. In fact, to our mutual shock, the rabbit's teeth didn't break my skin.

When the first rabbit tried to claw at my face, he had the same problem. Unfortunately, he also had a solution; he kicked me in the face. Magically impenetrable skin or not, it hurt.

I reached for my staff again, but one of the rabbits kicked me in the side of my abdomen, causing me to ball up in pain. By sheer determination, I didn't loosen my grip on my wand. I waved it at the carrot that was just out of reach, as the rabbits apparently wanted to fight me for it instead of just taking it. However, when magic shot from the wand and hit the carrot, tossing it high into the air, the rabbits focused on it instead. I had just enough time before it hit the ground to roll and grab my staff. *Attack.*

The staff obeyed my unspoken thought and blasted them with burning red energy. The rabbits turned to stone.

"*Where did you learn that?*" Merlin asked.

"I didn't. I remember reading something about it in one of Vactarus's books, but I didn't know how to do it. The staff did it."

"*If so, then the staff is much more powerful than I originally thought.*"

"So I can summon a monster now?"

"*Tend to your wounds and rest up. We will begin at first light.*"

Although my skin was still cold and impenetrable, the cuts that the rabbits caused before were still bleeding. "What do I do about it?"

"*Bandage it, of course.*"

"What about healing potions?"

"*By all means, if you know how to make one and can conjure the ingredients, do so,*" he said. I didn't know any, so he continued. "*You should ask Vac if he has any bandages and something to clean your cuts with. First, you need to release your spell. Do exactly as I told you before.*"

I sat down harder than I meant to and realized that I felt a little too heavy and pretty tired. It took longer without him telling me, but I did manage to imagine everything as I had before, and when I opened my eyes, I felt normal.

"*You learn quickly.*"

"Thank you. What did you get at the tournament to disguise my hair?"

"*I found a world traveler who had good black ink. That should last about five to seven days unless you wash your hair out. If nothing else, it might help you to appear more intimidating to Magnus or a villager.*"

"Yes, and if we run into my brothers again, I can hide my face and maybe they won't recognize me. I can put it in now."

"*Wait until we find out where the Island of Light is. We may be many days off and I only have enough to cover your hair once.*"

Merlin left and I returned to my room, where there was a bathtub set up with steaming water. And there was a dead girl in it.

"I'm sorry, did I come into the wrong room?" I asked, knowing I hadn't.

Kisha laughed. "No. I just wanted to talk to you and the bath was so inviting."

"How did it get here?" I was pretty sure I would have noticed a bathtub when I left that morning.

"The housekeeper brought it."

"Can you feel the warmth of the water?"

"No, but I can pretend. Come in."

"I don't think that would be a good idea. I'm going to the library to read." She didn't say anything, but she looked a little sad and lonely. "How long have you been a ghost?" I asked.

She looked at the water and shrugged her ghostly shoulders. "For longer than I can remember. I think this was my home originally. Vactarus named me Kisha because I couldn't remember my actual name."

"Do you remember how you died?" I asked. She shook her head. "Do you ever make it up?" She looked at me. "If you don't remember your own life, you can pretend. You could have been a dragon trainer or a wand maker."

She smirked. "Not likely. It's pretty obvious that I died young."

"That doesn't mean your life wasn't exciting."

"I guess you're right."

"Maybe you can even have an exciting afterlife. I'll try to think of something."

She smiled brightly. "I don't know why you want to be a sorcerer so much. You are a nicer man than anyone I know."

"It's not that I *want* to be a sorcerer. I *am* a sorcerer; I was born in a family of sorcerers. I'm just a failure as one, and there's no place in the world for someone who is a failure at being what they are."

"I would rather you be the way you are now than to change yourself. You haven't been here that long, but I liked you the first time you opened your mouth. That's special. Also, Vac trusts you to get his hat back. Vac doesn't trust anyone, and a sorcerer would use that against him. It's better to be a failed sorcerer than a failed friend." With those parting words, she vanished.

I considered taking a bath while the water was hot. After all, the housekeeper worked so hard to heat the water. Instead, I headed to the library to read up on conjuration. Access to such a grand library was worth a cold bath any day.

\*     \*     \*

Once again, I woke to a plate of eggs and potatoes. I barely had time to eat it before Merlin started calling me. With a sigh, I dressed and gathered my wand and staff. There was a bottle of ink outside my door, so I slipped it into my bag before heading out to the grassy field.

Merlin was already waiting. "Where are the rabbits?" I asked, hesitating when I saw that the statues were missing.

"*They reverted to normal overnight. Now, put your wand away, take your staff in both hands, and concentrate on your desire to defeat Magnus.*"

I did. *I will defeat the wizard and become someone nobody can doubt. I will never have to worry about my mother killing me for being an embarrassment to the family. I will be allowed to have books and do magic I want to do instead of curses and poisons.* The crystal of the staff began to glow, but it wasn't nearly as red as it had been the night before when I fought the rabbits. *I will be free of my mother…*

*No. I would just be a more powerful pawn of my mother's. She would kill me if I'm not useful to her, but she wouldn't just let me go if I became powerful enough to be useful.* The energy swirling in the crystal faded. *Defeating Magnus may be the only way to prove myself, but that's only the beginning. When I defeat him, I will have to face my mother.*

When I visualized Ilvera Dracre in my mind, the crystal burned deeper and redder than ever before and energy shot into the air. A figure began to take form, only to split into two shapes. I started to panic; I couldn't control two monsters if they turned on me!

Then, to my astonishment, the dark masses formed into two people standing right in front of me. It was a man and a woman, both of whom were dressed in the strangest clothes and studying me with even more curious expressions. Merlin growled, but they didn't seem to notice. Then, the woman looked out over the field. "I can see Russia from here!" she said excitedly.

The man in turn said, "Let's make Russia great again!"

"*Too evil!*" Merlin said, his growl deepening even more.

I knew that, though. Some part of me knew this was a disaster waiting to happen and that same part was reaching for my wand without thought. It was my wand that I used this time. White magic shot straight at them and with a burst of sparkles, they were gone.

"*That was easy,*" Merlin said.

"And oddly satisfying. Were they from another world?"

"*Yes.*"

"That poor world!"

"*Well, every world has its bad apples, I suppose. This time, use both your wand and your staff. They worked together last night to protect you. Come up with a creature you want and picture it in your head.*"

I thought of a bat first. However, as good as they were in warning people of danger, they weren't the best in attacking. Then I thought of a bear. They were big and powerful... *too powerful.* I couldn't control a bear. A monkey, on the other hand, was a good middle ground. They weren't too big and yet were very strong. Also, they were adorable in a weird way. "Okay, I know what I want to summon."

"*See it very clearly in your mind, and as you do, imagine there is a rope restraining it. This rope bounds its wrist and ankles, or tentacles, or whatever it has, and its neck.*"

I was fine until he said that; suddenly, my monkey had tentacles. I did bind them, though, as well as his limbs and neck.

*"If it has wings, make sure those are restrained."*

And just like that, the monkey had wings, too. I bound those clumsily.

*"Those ropes are all fed into your wand, so that you can control your beast by controlling your wand. Then, imagine the restraints are sinking deeper into the creature and becoming invisible. They're there, and they can still control the beast, but they cannot be seen or felt and it does not have to stay with you. You can call it to you, however. Because the ropes cannot be felt, they cannot break."*

This took some time. I wasn't an idiot; I wasn't going to rush this. Monkeys were strong, but my bloodline produced powerful sorcerers for many generations. I could do this. I would do this. The ropes in my mind embedded into the beast's limbs and around its neck. They would be controlled by my wand no matter how far away it is.

*"Now, hold that in your mind. Feel a sense of complete control, raise your wand in your left hand and your staff in your right, and call the beast to you."*

I did. Even though he didn't exist yet, I called him as if he did. Dark, red and black magic started glowing in the crystal of the staff.

Conjuring was vastly different than cursing or creating potions. Although I called it conjuring when I created food from clay, it was actually just transformation. Conjuring was on a whole other level. The body was created of the land and magic gave it life.

My mother never let me see the Dracre grimoires because she believed that sorcery was supposed to be passed down and she wanted to train us her way. She had never been interested in teaching us anything this powerful. Fortunately, I found several books on it in the library, so I had a general idea of what was happening. I knew I could affect the purpose of the creature by controlling what it was made of, but this method created more of a low-level, do-anything creature.

Bright red energy burst from the staff and white energy burst from the wand to form a crackling sphere of magic above me. Encouraged, I concentrated harder. Soon, the energy started darkening until it was black, after which it began to grow. As it grew larger, it became more solid, until it was the creature from my mind. My wand and staff stopped pouring magic into it.

The beast was dark brown, furry, and about the size of Merlin, with two arms and two legs. Although it looked skinny, I knew it had much more strength than any man. It also had two large, black, bat wings suspending it in the air and a row of four tentacles down each of its sides. The tentacles were black and writhing wildly. The creature itself studied me closely like it didn't know if I was dinner or not.

"*Control it before it gets away,*" Merlin cautioned.

I waved my wand at it. "Sit," I said. Its wings clamped shut and the poor beast hit the ground hard. I winced, but didn't go to it because it was still dangerous. "What do I do now?"

"*Banish it for now. Lock the power in your mind so that he is basically only in your head. Later, you can call him again and practice having him do something simple. You need to teach him to come when you call and that he is not to exist when you have no use for him.*"

"That seems a little harsh."

*"No more than making him sleep. Use your wand for this and set aside your staff."*

I nodded. My staff was unstable. Unfortunately, when I set it down, the crystal at the end flashed brightly and shot energy into the wand in my other hand, which vanished. "Oh, no."

Merlin sighed, and the creature took flight. When the beast dived threateningly at Merlin, I swung the staff instinctively. The creature got out of the way in time to avoid the blow and then flew off into the sky until I couldn't see him anymore.

"We have to find my wand." I knew it hadn't been destroyed; I always felt it when my mother disposed of my previous ones. "I have an idea, but you're not going to like it."

*"I have a premonition that I will feel that way about all of your ideas."*

\*　　\*　　\*

"So, let me get this straight. You found a magic staff with a dark and mysterious background and you used it. Each time, it was unpredictable and dangerous. Then you decided to create a monster using the staff and bind the monster to your wand. Once the monster had formed, your staff shot your wand and the wand vanished, effectively freeing the monster. Is that right?" Dessa asked.

"Well, when you put it that way, it sounds irresponsible."

Fortunately, the seer tournaments last for days, so we were able to return and find Dessa.

The seer sighed. "Obviously, your staff holds a power neither of you fully understand."

Merlin made a low growl. "*I am hundreds of years older than you, soothsayer.*"

Of course, Dessa couldn't hear him, and I wasn't about to insult her for him. "The only reason I can think of for your staff attacking your wand is that it was jealous you were using the wand."

I blinked, not sure I heard her correctly. "Jealous? How can a sorcerer staff be jealous?"

"Set it here on the table," she said.

I did, carefully. She opened a silver case where she kept one of her crystal balls, pulled out a pair of white silk gloves, and slipped them on. I felt uncomfortable when she ran her fingers delicately over the crystal, as if I was afraid she would break it. Then her eyes turned white, the crystal pulsed with a dim glow, and my skin crawled.

When she finally let go, I stepped between her and the staff. "So, do you know where I can find my wand?"

"I do. Your mother is the only sorceress known to have slayed a dragon."

"Actually, she was just trying to train... never mind."

"The staff has sent your wand to---"

"I'm not fighting a dragon," I interrupted.

"No. It sent your wand to the ruins of a castle that was brought down by dragons. Your wand is hidden in a mound of treasure and is drawing in the monster you created. Thus, you must go and fight your own creation to retrieve your wand."

"Lovely. Dying was absolutely on my list of things to do today."

# CHAPTER 7

"It's just a shortcut."

"*We should stay on the road,*" Merlin argued, eyeing the dark forest with suspicion.

"But that will take an entire day. Maybe even two!"

"*If we get lost, it will take even longer.*"

"You're a wolf. Are you saying you can't find your way out of the forest?" I asked. He glared at me, but I headed into it before he could argue again. Since I was not going to be around other people for a while, I took off my robe and put it in my bag.

It was a little darker than the average forest, which was why it was called the Dark Forest, but I had never had any trouble when I went through it. Well, there was the time a troll captured me and took me back to his cave to eat me. I escaped by setting his entire cave on fire. Fortunately, it wasn't troll season this time.

It was also not as hot inside and the shade was a definite relief. We traveled for a while without incident.

"So, will you tell me why me being the seventh son is significant?" I asked when the silence became uncomfortable. I didn't hear birds, bugs, or anything, and that wasn't normal.

*"I suppose I should. Because seven is regarded as a magical number, it is said that the seventh son of the seventh son will have natural abilities in magic, as long as the line is not broken by daughters or death. How that affects you, with your sorcery, I cannot be sure."*

"Wouldn't that mean I should have more magic than the rest of my family?"

*"Quite possibly. However, seven is not sinister, so the seventh son should not be inherently corrupt."*

"Wait, so I'm this way because I was the seventh born?"

*"Not completely. It did not make you inherently good, either. I have always believed a person's kindness was a derivative of nurture over nature, but knowing your mother, you might just be the exception."*

"What?"

*"I said I do not know why you are nice."*

"So why didn't you just say that before?"

*"I believe your mother married your father because he was the seventh son of his line with the intention of stealing your power."*

"She never said anything to me about the seventh son having more magic. Besides, stealing someone's magic is not that easy. There's no way my mother would risk having a child who was more powerful than her."

*"Have you ever heard of someone named Livia?"*

"Isn't that who Vactarus mentioned?"

*"You have an impressive memory. Like you, she was born to a family of sorcerers and she could do both light and dark magic. Unlike you, however, she embraced her magic."*

"I can do sorcery, I'm just not good at it."

*"So you believe the problem is that your curses always go awry and not that you can only produce light magic?"*

"I... well... I think it's both. Sometimes, I can do a curse, but if I do manage dark magic, it still ends up helping someone. Otherwise, my magic just twists what I say around to do something nice."

*"How are you with fire? Can you set a fire?"*

"Usually. Sometimes I have to do it without magic, though."

*"Sometimes?"*

"Well... when it's for personal gain."

*"So, when it is sorcery then,"* he said. I nodded. He stopped and indicated a certain tree with his paw. *"Set that tree on fire."*

"No way! It's just a poor tree."

*"It is a dead tree. There are no leaves on its branches. I suspect a parasite, in which case, you could be saving the trees around it by burning it."*

"Or it could burn down the forest."

*"Thus, proving you are capable of sorcery."*

I groaned and aimed the staff at the tree. I imagined the dead branches on fire, illuminating the darkness of the forest, while also hoping deep down that I didn't set the forest on fire. Magic flowed from me into the staff. Right before I could give the command to my magic, Merlin tensed and his fur started bristling. "What's wrong?"

*"Something is watching us."*

"Seriously? What is it? I am absolutely not fighting a dragon. If I see one, I'm going to gawk and coo and try to pet it. Unless it tries to eat me. If it tries to eat me, I'm going to run and then think back on the occasion fondly."

*"You are rambling."*

"Of course I'm rambling!"

*"Stay here,"* he said before disappearing into the cover of some thorn bushes.

"Great. Now who am I supposed to ramble to?" I listened for anything odd aside from the fact that there was no sound at all. With each moment, I grew more nervous. It occurred to me that we should have stayed on the main road.

*"Ayden, run,"* Merlin said.

"What? What's going on?" I asked.

He didn't answer, but I heard growling and snapping. The sound of an animal snapping its teeth was unmistakable. I ran towards the sound. Before I could see Merlin, however, I tripped. When I tried to stand, something wrapped around my ankles and pulled.

I looked down, saw thick vines making their way up my legs, and knew what trouble I was in. "Oh, gods." I reached inside my bag for the knife I always kept in it, but ended up dropping the sack and my staff as the vines hoisted me up into the air by my feet. "Merlin… can you help?"

It was silent for a moment.

*"Not really."* His voice sounded strained even in my head.

Realizing that his hearing was much better than mine, I spoke at a normal volume. "Are you tied up, too?"

*"Yes. Once we know what we are up against, we can---"*

"I know what we're up against, and there's not much we can do. I've faced these beings before." Actually, I'd been captured by them before, but it really wasn't my fault. It was my brothers who tied me to a tree in the middle of Blue Lakes Forest.

"Well, well, it's not every day two wizards intrude into our forests," an unseen voice hissed. I heard Merlin growling again, but I still couldn't see him.

"I'm not a wizard. I'm a sorcerer! And Merlin is a wolf."

"He may be cursed, but we can see he is a wizard, as we can see you are no sorcerer."

I crossed my arms and glared at nothing in particular. I probably didn't look that intimidating with my blond hair blowing in the slight breeze and all my blood rushing into my face. I was going to have a massive headache from this. "You want to come out here, let me grab my staff, and say that to my face?"

"You are a foolish wizard." Despite his answer, he hopped down from a nearby tree. If he stood next to me right-side-up, his head would barely reach my chest. He was also very slender, fine-boned, wearing clothes made of leaves and vines, and had pointed ears. His hair was dark brown, long, and braided, while his eyes were the same mixture of brown and green as the forest. His complexion was darker than the elves of Blue Lakes Forest.

"I haven't done anything to you or your forest, so just call off your vines and let me and Merlin go."

More elves came out of hiding— at least two dozen. The first one, who was probably their king, narrowed his eyes at me. "I have had enough problems with sorcerers lately. If I let you go free, more wizards will follow."

"I told you I'm not---" I stopped myself when I realized what he said. "Wait, what problems with sorcerers?"

He scowled. "Sorcerers passed through here just yesterday. Six of them! Do you know how many animals they hunted and foliage they ruined?! Worst of all, they cursed my daughter when she wasn't enamored by them."

"Six sorcerers? Did they all happen to have black hair, wine-colored eyes, and green robes?"

"Yes!" he hissed. All of the other elves hissed with him, creating a creepy echo effect.

*My brothers were here*? I changed my opinion of him instantly, since I knew why the elves were so irritable. There was nothing my brothers could do better than irritate someone. "Listen, those sorcerers are the Dracre sons. They're my enemies, too."

His scowl faded a little. "So, you expect me to let you go because we share a common enemy?"

"I would hope so."

"I am not in a merciful mood."

"Once they get what they're after, they're going to turn around and come back this way. I won't hurt anything in the forest; I don't even hunt. I eat apples and broccoli mostly. Merlin hunts, but he doesn't eat much and we're in too much of a hurry. Besides, he doesn't have any magic. You have nothing to lose by letting us go and we could stop those sorcerers from coming back."

"I want them to come back. I will force them to retract the curse on my daughter."

I grimaced. "What kind of curse?"

"They turned her into a tree," he hissed. Again, the other elves echoed the creepy sound.

I sighed internally with relief. "That would be Gibus's doing. I can break it." Whereas my other brothers preferred illnesses and embarrassing curses, Gibus tried to be ironic. He had also cursed pretty much every woman in Akadema for not immediately throwing herself at his feet. Undoing his work was always left up to me.

He narrowed his eyes. "How?" he asked, unconvinced.

"I'm looking for my wand, which is in the ruins of a castle about a day's walk north. That's why we wanted to come through the forest; we wanted to get it before the Dracre sons get to their destination. It looks like we're really behind, though."

"I know the castle ruins of which you speak."

"Once I get my wand, I'll come back here. I can break Gibus's tree curse any day, but I need my wand to do it."

"What guarantee do I have that you will come back if I let you go?"

"Keep the other wizard," one of the elves suggested.

I tried to glare at him, but I couldn't tell which one had spoken. "Merlin is no one's collateral." I had every intention of returning to break Gibus's curse, but I had no idea how to defeat the monster. I also didn't like ultimatums.

"*When they let you go, grab your staff and curse them,*" Merlin suggested.

That was what any sorcerer would have done, but I had no idea what my staff would do or how many elves were still camouflaged and hiding. Also, Merlin must not have had elves where he was from, because everyone knew how powerful they were. Their magic was tied to nature, as seen with the vines. Arrows and spears were their primary method of defense, but they were clever. I could curse a few of them and it would stick, but I didn't know what my staff would do, and I certainly couldn't stop every single elf in the forest simultaneously.

"If you truly mean to come back and help us, then you should be willing to leave your companion."

"Merlin?" I asked, wishing once again that I could speak in his mind like he could mine. "Can you still hear me?"

"*Yes, I can hear you both.*"

"Are you okay with staying here?"

"*Absolutely not.*"

"He says it's okay," I told the elves. Showing them that we trusted them would go a long way towards convincing them to trust us, even if we didn't really trust them.

He nodded to one of the other elves and a moment later, the vines slowly lowered me to the ground and finally released my ankles. I stayed down. Although my brothers saw submission as encouragement to torture their victim more, the elves were a reasonable race.

"Go then, and return with your wand by sunrise to break the curse over my daughter."

"I will return, but if you hurt Merlin, even a little bit, I will tear every one of you to pieces and burn your forest down on top of you." I grabbed my staff and bag and stood. The elves looked surprised. "Merlin, I'll be back before sunrise."

"*You had better be,*" he said. "*For the record, this is not how a sorcerer behaves.*"

*     *     *

Even though I walked as fast as I could, it was dark by the time I reached the main road on the other side of the forest, and the warm afternoon had turned into a cold night. I put my robe back on. Fortunately, I could walk faster on the clear path.

Soon, I came upon the decrepit ruins of what was once a grand castle... surrounded by homes. I groaned. Fighting the monster to get my wand back and getting treasure in return was one thing, but sorcerers were not supposed to save people. Then again, I created the beast, so I was responsible for the damage it caused.

I sighed. "Nobody can tell Merlin ever," I said aloud.

The houses were small, well-built, and in most cases, on fire. I spared a moment to hope that the creature I created wasn't a fire-breather before I headed into the thick of the mess. What few people that hadn't already fled were frantically trying to gather their valuables and put out fires.

I caught the arm of a man running past me. "Good evening. Sorry to interrupt your panicking, but can you please tell me that you are being attacked by a dragon... or maybe a werewolf?" *Anything that I didn't create.*

He straightened his shirt to appear more dignified, but the fact that his sleeves were burned off and he was carrying a sack of grain in his arms like a baby defeated the purpose. "Actually, we were attacked by a flying monkey with tentacles."

*Great.* I had to get my wand, but saving these people after creating a monster that attacked their village was the last thing any sorcerer in the world would do. If my mother was here, she would be proud that I was finally able to cause mayhem and tell me not to worry about my wand. I had a staff, after all.

But she wasn't here, and I couldn't just let the monster run rampant. I created him, and it was my fault he got free. I wanted to be a sorcerer, I really did, but this had been a mistake, and even sorcerers owned up to their mistakes.

Although the castle could still be identified as such, several walls had been blown out by dragons. I entered the ruins through one of the massive holes in the side. On the ground floor, weeds had grown up through the cracks in the stone and wrapped around the old furniture. Almost everything wooden was molded, including some paintings from the original family who owned the place. It was dark, but moonlight streamed in through holes in the roof and fire from the nearby homes provided eerie, flickering light that made it look like things were moving.

*Where would the treasure be? That is where I'll find my wand and the monster.* My father used to tell me that some dragons liked caves, and some liked heights, which didn't help at all. I either needed to find the dungeons or the tallest tower. There were five doors and two sets of stairs, suggesting that randomly searching this place could take much longer than I had. I couldn't hear the monster, either.

I dropped my bag and started to put down my staff to get my knife out when I got an idea. I held out my staff. "You got us into this mess. Show me where my wand is." Nothing happened. "Fine," I snarled at it. "Show me where the treasure is. If you don't, you're worthless to me and I'll leave you here."

I felt the staff pulling on my magic before the crystal lit with a red glow. Just that. I was just about to put it down and grab my knife when the glow in the crystal narrowed to form a beam of light that pointed to one of the two sets of stairs.

"Wow. I didn't think that would actually work." Before the staff could change its mind, I grabbed my bag and hurried up the stairs. On the second floor, the beam of light changed to point down the hall, where there was another staircase. Unfortunately, each floor was more dangerous than the previous. By the time I reached the last staircase, there were sections of it smashed so badly I had to balance on the handrail to get past it.

The top floor was deplorable. There was a gaping chasm in the middle of the hallway. Most of the ceiling was gone, many walls had crumbled, and there was water damage on pretty much everything. I could see into many of the old bedrooms as I passed them and could only tell what they were by the fact that they had remnants of beds in them.

I didn't, however, find any treasure. "Where is it?" I asked the staff. The beam of light spilled across the floor and over the chasm. "Figures. Why isn't the monster attacking?" Surely he knew that if I found my wand, I could control him. The staff didn't answer.

I examined the gap in the floor until I had a firm plan. I went into the closest room and found a broken bed leg. Then, I pulled some rope out of my bag, tied one end around the middle of the leg, and wedged the leg into the debris left of the wall. I tied the other end of the rope around myself and tossed my bag and staff across the gap. The wall beside the chasm had holes knocked out, so I used those to climb across. The rope was just for emergency. Fortunately, I made it to the other side with only a couple small slipups that took years off my life. I untied the rope and set a rock on the end so that I could use it to get back.

When I picked up my staff again, the beam of light resumed… and led right out the window. I knew whatever it was would be bad, but I had no idea how bad. Outside the window was a tower. Across from me was a large window in the tower with part of a broken bridge hanging out of it. From my angle, I couldn't see any way into the tower except through this window. Unfortunately, I was running out of time. Through the tower window, I could just make out the dull glint of gold.

*How am I supposed to get over there*? I could have used Merlin's advice. Since I didn't have his help, I relied on what I did have. I dug through my bag, looking for a plan. I could throw a rock over with a rope attached, but I couldn't throw one heavy enough to hold my weight. *But maybe my staff can.*

Just as I raised my staff to try something, the building shook and I heard the eerie howl of a monkey. My skin grew numb as the staff made me impenetrable again. At least, I hope that's what it was doing. Unfortunately, that wouldn't protect me from being crushed under rocks.

Before I could even think up a spell, the floor started to collapse, and I ended up rolling straight into the chasm. Fortunately, I caught the rope and saved myself from plummeting to my death. The rope held my weight and I held on no matter how much my hands hurt, because right below me, my monster was fighting none other than a huge brown bear.

And the bear was losing.

My staff fell to the ground harmlessly. I considered pushing away from the wall and letting go so that I could land near my staff, but when a swipe of the bear's paw nearly got me in the abdomen, I started climbing the rope instead. And I nearly got to the top.

Then the rope snapped, and I landed right between the monster and the bear. For one precious moment, they stared at me in shock. The bear then leaned over me until his face was so close to mine that I could feel his hot breath. I would have stopped myself from gagging if I weren't trying so hard to control my other bodily functions. When the bear opened his mouth wide, displaying all his sharp teeth, I forgot to breathe altogether.

And then he sneezed on my face.

I made a sound I had never made before; it was something like a shriek of disgust, but with my eyes and mouth closed. I heard the bear's roar of pain at the same time I felt him being thrown off me. I sat up and reached for my staff just as the bear was tossed backwards into it. Although the staff rolled away unscathed, I had to dive out of the way. The monster was tearing at him viciously. I once again tried to get to my staff. It was now in the far corner, balancing dangerously on the edge of yet another hole in the floor. If the monster or bear were slammed to the floor again, my staff would fall.

The monster's sharp claws tried to swipe at me as I passed, but the bear was closer and apparently faster. His front paw smacked into me from behind and I was propelled towards my staff, away from the monster. I landed rolling and went with it. The wall stopped my fall just as my staff began tipping into the hole. I pounced, knowing already that it was too late, because it was gone before I could reach the hole.

But my body apparently didn't know that, and I had my legs braced and my entire upper body through the hole before I knew what I was doing. I caught it. Barely.

Gasping with relief and exertion, I climbed out of the hole and wiped sweat from my face. With the fighting bear and monster in front of me, I had every intention of running out of the castle and trying to find another way into the tower. Unfortunately, that was when the bear roared in pain. The monster had its claws around the bear's front paws to prevent him from attacking and its tentacles were around the bear's throat.

A sorcerer was ruthless, manipulative, and self-centered. That was what my family was and that was what they expected me to be. Unlike my brothers, however, I didn't think that included cruelty to animals. I might not have risked my life for the bear if I hadn't created the monster myself… but I probably would have.

Darting around the monster, I grabbed one end of the rope. I didn't have a plan so much as a terrible idea that would never work. That was pretty much my life. With the staff in hand, I ducked under the monster's arm and tentacles to put myself between it and the bear, then thrust the crystal of the staff towards the monster's chest.

"Get back," I demanded.

The monster did, though it was only from surprise that I would stand up to it. One of its claws swiped at my arm, but my staff's magic protected my skin. I felt my magic bonding with the staff again as if even my magic knew I was being threatened.

I realized then what Dessa had meant. My staff was not just a tool of magic; it had its own awareness. It wasn't like mine or another person's, but it was enough that the staff knew what was happening. As the staff's energy mingled with mine, it felt like it was trying to get to know me. As if it was trying to determine if I was a worthy master.

That was really depressing, because I knew it would find me unfit, since it was a sorcerer staff and I was bad at sorcery. Here I was, putting myself in danger to save a bear.

*Don't think about that. I have to do this. I will do this. Merlin is counting on me.* The crystal started glowing more fiercely than I had ever seen it, but it was also lighter red. The monster sneered at me and his tentacles reached forth to take the staff from me. That wasn't going to happen. The harmless glow swelled out of the crystal and struck as lightning.

With a cry of pain, the creature was thrown back. I winced, sympathetic and even a little apologetic, because I had created it in the first place, and now I was attacking it for following its basic instincts.

When it got back up, I waved the staff at it. Instead of attacking me, the creature took flight. Fortunately, my staff knew what to do; the other end of the rope shot up and wrapped around the monkey monster's leg. He flew up, to the top floor, and out the window, dragging me out with him. Of course, when the beast flew from one window to the window of the tower, I fell. I was expecting it, though, so I held on and put my legs out to stop myself from crashing into the wall. It went perfectly; my legs braced me and the further into the tower the monkey went, the more he pulled me up and towards the window. Soon, I was over the lip of the window, balancing on the edge between safety and certain death. If the monster came at me instead of flying further away, I would have fallen. I just had to not look down.

"Oh, gods," I moaned when I saw the ground so far beneath me.

The monster jerked suddenly and tossed me inside, where I landed face-first in gold coins and jewels. It hurt, but it meant that I was on solid ground, so I was okay with it. I started to get up, only to have to roll out of the way as the monkey dived at me. Lightning shot from my staff again, but the monster dodged it.

"Where is the wand?" I asked my staff. It didn't answer me, so I dug through the piles of treasure while evading the monster and shooting him with lightning whenever he got too close. He was no longer trying to claw me; he was learning. When he tried to drop a massive wooden chest on me, I gave up on my wand and faced the beast. "What is wrong with you?" I asked him. "I created you to help me."

This time, he didn't dive at me or move away. In fact, he was staring at my staff expectantly.

"What?" I closed my eyes, praying that he wouldn't strike at that exact moment, and focused on the sensation of my magic flowing inside me and in the staff. The staff wasn't doing magic itself, but it was certainly doing *something*. I opened my eyes and imagined the restraints around the monkey's limbs and neck.

Although I could see them clearly in my mind, it wasn't what I expected. The restraints to his limbs and wings all combined into one rope that led to a pile of gold

I hadn't checked, but the rope around his neck was tied to the crystal in my staff. Suddenly, I understood.

"I get it. I bet it's hurting you, isn't it? The wand is pulling you here and the staff is pulling you towards me. You probably don't want me controlling you, but you don't want it to hurt, either." I moved towards the wand and the monkey snarled. I snarled back in attempt to show him I wasn't going to submit and reached into the pile of gold. My wand felt warm when I pulled it out and the relief I felt bordered on irrational. It was as if I had lost something very important to me that I finally got back.

With both my wand and staff in hand, I turned back to the monkey, who landed before me. I wished Merlin had shown me how to banish the creature before I came after it. "I banish you. Whether that means you leave or cease to exist, you are not allowed to hurt anyone. Don't worry; I'll call you soon and you'll have the opportunity to cause destruction then. Go, and don't return until I call you."

He closed his wings around him and dispersed. He just sort of poofed out of existence, but in a slow and detailed way.

And then the tower rumbled and shook. Acting on instinct, I ran to the window just as the tower started to tilt towards the castle. Right before the tower actually crashed into the wall of the castle, I jumped from one window to the next. Because of the momentum and the narrower distance, I made it, but the tower still crashed, and since there was very little roof left, that all came down on top of me. I allowed myself to fall from one floor to the next to stay ahead of the destruction, but as I started falling faster and faster, everything became a blur. I couldn't stop myself and between me falling on sharp objects and heavy objects falling on me, there was no telling how many bones I broke.

After a while, I became aware that everything was still, although I had no idea how much time had passed. I was lying under a pile of rocks and dirt in a beam of light with no idea whether it was sunlight or moonlight. Then I saw one bear paw reaching out of the dark for me, and I passed out.

# CHAPTER 8

I woke in a lot less pain than I had been expecting. Actually, I was just glad to be waking at all. When I opened my eyes, I found myself in a warm, dark hut, on a soft bed instead of a pile of rocks in the castle. Something was on my forehead, but it was cool and felt good, so I didn't try to move it.

"Rest. You are still healing." Even though the voice was soft and feminine, it made my head hurt.

"What happened?" I asked, trying to see the person without moving my head. There was a man sitting in a nearby chair, but he was asleep.

A woman stepped into my line of vision. She was short and a little plump with dark blue robes. Although her hair was a smattering of silver and gray, her face and eyes looked way too young for her hair to have turned. It was oddly unsettling.

"You were gravely injured while saving the town."

I tried to sit up, but she pushed against my shoulders and I was overcome with nausea. "My wand and staff," I said. My voice was scratchy. The staff's spell to protect me was also gone.

"Bralyn got them. Your staff, wand, and bag are right here. You need to sleep and heal."

I didn't know who Bralyn was, but it reminded me who was counting on me. "How long have I been here?"

"Not long. I gave you a healing potion that should have you back together by sunrise."

That explained things; she was a mage. "It isn't sunrise yet? Thank the gods. I have to go. I have to get to the Dark Forest by sunrise."

"There is no possible way you could make it."

"I will. I don't know what they'll do to Merlin if I'm not back, but elves won't be merciful if I break a promise."

"I don't understand," she said as I pulled the wet cloth off my head and struggled out of bed.

Vertigo made standing much more difficult than it should have been. Fortunately, the mage understood that I had something important to do, so she picked my stuff up and handed them to me, then helped me out of the hut. Outside, I faced a wall of villagers, who all hollered with delight.

The sudden noise stabbed at my headache like a knife between my ears. My stomach rebelled, but since there was nothing to expel, I didn't have to worry about puking in front of everyone. I've been there and done that; it was highly embarrassing. "What's happening?" I asked, still not able to get my voice right.

"When you destroyed the beast and brought down the tower, the treasure from the ancient dragons spilled out into the village. You made everyone rich along with saving us. I have never met a braver wizard."

"I'm not a wizard, I'm a… never mind." I didn't have the energy to explain. "I have to get to the Dark Forest." The sky was already starting to lighten. I knew that I would never make it, especially since I was injured.

I tried to think of a spell, a curse, *anything*, that could help me. When I felt a nudge in my back, I ignored it. Then I had to duck out of the way before a sharp horn could impale my shoulder. "Not you again!" I said, exasperated. The unicorn was back. "Why do you follow me every…" I stopped and stroked his head as I realized what this meant. I couldn't make it back to Merlin on time by foot, but surely a unicorn could. "Can you help me? I need to get to the Dark Forest elves by sunrise."

The unicorn tossed his head and knelt.

"Thank you." I had to have help getting on and even then I couldn't sit up without a struggle. Obviously, the potion had a lot more work to do, because I wasn't strong enough to hold three items. Making a quick decision, I tossed the bag to the ground and pocketed my wand. The bag had been mine for as long as I could remember, but Merlin needed help.

As soon as I was relatively secure, the unicorn took off at a gallop.

With every passing moment, the sky grew lighter and I grew stronger. By the time we reached the forest, sunlight was touching the tips of the trees. The unicorn was undeterred. He glided over roots and bushes that I would have struggled with, and I knew we would make it. We came to a clearing with only a single, small apple tree in the middle of it. He didn't slow before stopping suddenly in front of the tree, but my blood felt alive like it only did when I faced death. I jumped down from the unicorn easily and pulled my wand from my pocket.

"I'm here. Release Merlin," I demanded. Elves suddenly appeared from the depths of the forest and tops of the trees. Most of them were difficult to differentiate, so I was only guessing that it was their king who stopped right in front of me.

"You returned on time. I will release your companion, but you must break the curse on my daughter."

"Where is she?" I asked. He pointed to the apple tree. I should have guessed; it wasn't like any of the other trees and for some reason, Gibus often compared women to apples. When the elven king took another step towards me, the unicorn tossed its head at him, as if telling him to get back.

I set my staff down on the ground, aimed my wand at the tree, and envisioned the tree like a shell around a small woman. *Return her to normal.* I imagined the tree cracking and falling away from her. When my magic shot through the wand, I encountered Gibus's magic in the tree. That was expected and fortunately, I've broken his curses many times.

I let my magic settle over his like a blanket to feel out the weak points. There were always weak points because my brother's intentions were shallow. Although he liked the flashy curses, like this one, he was absentminded and impatient, so the weak points were often in the details. That meant the leaves, branches, and roots in this case. In fact, the only stronghold he had on the curse was the trunk. I tore at his energy from the top and bottom until it frayed like a badly sewn sweater.

What everyone else saw was the tree melting into a pretty little elven girl with long gold hair and green eyes. It was apparently not as easy as I had thought, though, because I was slightly out of breath when I was done. Nevertheless, healing potions always left me with a little too much energy, so I wasn't in any danger.

The elf king went to his daughter and hugged her. "You are much more powerful than we had thought," he told me.

"Where is Merlin?"

He made a motion with his hands and I heard a vine snap. A moment later, Merlin emerged from the darkness. At least I knew why this forest was given its name; even in daylight, it was mostly dark.

"We will hereby consider you a friend and if you cross our path again, we will make sure you have a safe passage."

"I appreciate that. You don't happen to know where I can find the Island of Light, do you?"

"No; we stay in the forest. I do know there is no Island of Light on Akadema."

They all vanished into the trees. "*Explain*," Merlin said.

"Later." The forest had ears.

\*     \*     \*

Fortunately, we made it the rest of the way without getting attacked, captured, or eaten. Instead of returning to Vactarus's mansion, we decided to go past the village I had just saved since my brothers went that way. Most likely, they knew the right way and our best bet was to follow them until we had a clue where we were going.

I didn't want to overtax the unicorn after he helped me so much, so I walked instead of riding on him. Unfortunately, as soon as we emerged from the forest, he pranced off in his own direction. It was getting too warm for my robe by then, but I didn't have a bag to put it in.

"I'm hungry," I said.

Merlin sighed. *"Then explain to me why you insisted that I not hunt us some food."*

"Because the Dark Forest elves would have strung us back up and left us for the animals to eat. My brothers have been through here and the elves weren't happy about their hunting any more than they were them turning their king's daughter into a tree. How much of our conversation did you hear?"

*"All of it, including that you vowed to return for me and break their curse. That was very noble of you. A sorcerer would have cursed them and escaped with or without me."*

"I wouldn't have left you." I wasn't expecting his thoughtful frown... probably because he was a wolf. "Would you have left me?"

*"Probably not."*

"Well, the elves thought that I was a wizard, which worked in our favor this once."

*"This once? I know that sorcerers are respectable and accepted members of society here, but people generally prefer wizards to sorcerers."*

I gaped. "No way! Wizards are too pretentious, not to mention they're just as self-centered as sorcerers, only with slightly different values."

*"Vastly different values, and no, they are not as selfish as sorcerers. I had already guessed that it was your brothers who cursed the elf's daughter, so tell me what happened when you went after your*

*wand. You were gone for a long time, but you appear to be uninjured."*

So, I explained everything, including that the castle ruins had people around it. I left out the part about saving a bear, though. I mean, how could that possibly be important? Merlin was quiet for a while, no doubt deciding that there was no way I would ever be a proper sorcerer. "If I had been able to take some of the gold, at least that would have been selfish."

*"The point is that you saved people and gave them the gold they could never get their hands on. You do realize that was the last thing a sorcerer would have done, right?"*

"Yes, I know. Are you disappointed?"

*"Why would I be disappointed?"*

"My family would be horrified."

*"Remember that I am from a world where there is no such distinction between wizards and sorcerers. I agreed to teach you how to be a sorcerer, not force you to be one. You know very well what was right and what was wrong. You made a choice and I have no right to be disappointed when any sorcerer would have left me to fend for myself. Now, conjure some food. I am hungry enough to eat apples."*

We stopped walking. "Maybe I can conjure some tofu."

*"Apples,"* he insisted.

"Well, I can't just conjure food out of thin air. I need something edible that I can transform."

"You transformed clay into food on the night you released me from the syrus," he pointed out.

"That's different. That was special transformation clay. It's like emergency food, and I'm out of it."

"Hello there!" a man called, coming down the road towards us.

I frowned when I realized he looked oddly familiar. Merlin glanced at me. "*Is he a friend of yours?*"

I shook my head. "I've seen him before, but I don't remember where."

"*Is that not your bag?*" he asked.

Only then did I realize the man was carrying my satchel. He was tall and heavily built with the type of muscles only generation-bred warriors had. When he got close enough, I recognized the shoulder-length, dark brown hair and the scruffy goatee on his face. "You're the man who was asleep in the mage's hut," I said. I also noticed that he had a very large sword at his side and intentionally didn't bring it up. "That's a really big sword." *Oops.* My mouth wasn't as wise as my brain.

He grinned brightly, stopped in front of me, and held out my bag. "I'm Bralyn, and I was the one who pulled you out of the castle." Then he sneezed. Before he could compose himself, he sneezed five more times.

"Are you okay?" I asked.

He backed away. "I'm sorry, but the wind just changed direction. I'm allergic to fur."

"Allergic to fur? Well, thank you for bringing me my bag." I tried to take it from him, but he didn't hand it over.

"I haven't just come to bring your bag to you; I want to help you on your quest."

"Why do you think I'm on a quest?" I asked.

He frowned at me. "I know the look of someone on a mission."

"You don't even know what mission it is."

"No, but I'm a warrior; quests are what I do. I was sent to destroy the monkey monster, but you did it instead.

I can't return to my guild empty-handed. As far as I'm concerned, your quest is mine as well now."

"*Seriously?*" Merlin asked.

"This is Merlin, and he's helping me, so if you're allergic to fur, I really don't see any way you can help."

"It shouldn't be a problem as long as I stand upwind of him."

"*Tell him where we are going. He will not want to face a powerful wizard.*"

"I'm trying to defeat Magnus."

"The Great Wizard? That is a tricky one, because his castle is extremely difficult to find."

"That's our problem. We're looking for a place called the Island of Light, and---"

"Oh, right between the Shimmering Isles and Ghost Mountain."

"You know where the Island of Light is?" I asked, gaping.

"Yes. I live at the base of Ghost Mountain in a city called Red Rock. My friends and I used to swim to the Island of Light when we were little."

"Great! Can you show us the way?"

"I will take you there myself."

I knew having a warrior helping us was a huge advantage, even if he was allergic to Merlin. Aside from the fact that they were trained their entire lives to fight, they were courageous and clever. I could learn something. "I would appreciate the help."

Bralyn started leading us back the way he had come, toward the castle ruins. "Just out of curiosity, though… why are you trying to defeat Magnus? Aren't wizards usually on the same side?"

I sighed. "I'm not a wizard, I'm a sorcerer."

"Really? Aren't you a little... small to be a sorcerer?"

"No, I'm not. I'm going to defeat Magnus to prove that."

If anything, this seemed to brighten Bralyn's mood even more. "Fantastic! There is nothing I understand better than a quest to prove yourself. To win or lose to an honorable opponent is a rare treat, and only by defeating those who are stronger than you can you become a better man."

"*A better fighter, yes, but it takes many qualities to make you a man,*" Merlin argued. Of course, Bralyn couldn't hear him and I ignored him. "*He is hiding something. There is something very odd about his scent, though I cannot identify it.*"

I didn't respond, since I wasn't sure if it was a good idea or not to reveal that Merlin was a wizard and not just a wolf. Keeping that a secret would make the trip pretty awkward.

Bralyn was in a good mood, which I thought was unusual. Although I had never personally met a warrior, I was under the impression that they were all very serious and short-tempered. They were primarily sent out on quests to fight monsters and people who get too powerful and destructive. They were not often assigned to guard castles because they tended to be too impulsive and restless. While warriors were independent, they were part of the warrior's guild and had to work their way up in the ranks to receive the better quests. Mages, magical healers, were the main providers of the quests.

My stomach rumbled. When Bralyn pulled out a loaf of bread and handed it to me, it took everything in me not to make a loud sound of delight. I started to break off some for Merlin, but he took off running into the long grass to our right. It took me a moment to realize he was hunting some small mammal.

"I've never seen a real wolf before," Bralyn said quietly. "I thought they were extinct."

"Well, Merlin is special."

"How so?"

I hesitated. "I think if I told you, you wouldn't help us find the Island of Light."

"A warrior never breaks his oath. I vow to help you get there."

"Why are you so adamant?"

"As I said before, you defeated the monster I was sent to destroy. I need to complete a mission before I can return home without shame."

He was lying. "How did you know about the monster? He was only created yesterday."

"We have a seer in our guild. And how do you know when the monster was... wait... created? It was conjured by a sorcerer? How do you know that?"

"Well... I'm the one who conjured it. I'm Ayden Dracre and my mother---"

"You're a Dracre?" he interrupted.

"I guess you've heard of us. I shouldn't be surprised. Yes, my family is well-known for their sorcery, but I'm a complete failure at it. Before I got my staff, I only had my wand, which couldn't do black magic. I overheard my brothers saying that my mother was sending them after Magnus, and that I wasn't going. My mother would rather kill me than allow me to be an embarrassment to the family, so I knew the only way I could prove myself was to defeat Magnus before my brothers could."

"So you're going to go and fight a wizard you have never met just because you're afraid of your mother?"

"You obviously have no idea what it's like to be ridiculed your entire life. My brothers have buried me alive, cursed me, burned me, cut me, stabbed me, and left me for dead in the most dangerous places on Akadema, and my mother encouraged it. I'm more afraid of Ilvera Dracre than Magnus."

"Actually, that makes sense. I would much rather be killed by a wizard than a sorceress," he said thoughtfully. "And I have had my share of ridicule as well." I arched an eyebrow in disbelief. "I'm allergic to *fur*. Of course I've been ridiculed."

"But you're a warrior. I thought warriors kill everyone who dishonors them."

"We are still people, just like sorcerers and wizards are people. Yes, we are nothing without our honor. We are raised to handle all kinds of stress in order to stand strong before our enemy, and that includes being tormented with our weaknesses."

"Then I am stronger because my brothers harassed me?"

"I suspect so. I would rather face an enemy with a fellow survivor than someone who was never tested. How does the wolf come in to this?"

"A few days ago, I somehow released Merlin from a magical box and it turns out he's actually a wizard from another world who can talk to me in my head because I was the one who released him. He agreed to teach me to be a sorcerer, yet I still keep screwing up. I tried to create a monster to help me and control it with my wand, but the wand disappeared and I had to get it back in order to control the monster. A seer told me where the wand was, but not that there were people at the ruins."

"So it wasn't your plan to save everyone and shower the town with the dragon treasure?"

"No, that was an accident."

"And why wasn't Merlin with you?"

"He was being held hostage by the Dark Forest elves and I had to get back by sunrise with my wand to break the curse that one of my brothers put on the elf king's daughter."

"Right. Sorcerer or not, you are the oddest person I have ever met."

Merlin came back with blood on his snout. *"Before we reach his castle, you need a plan to defeat Magnus."*

I nodded. "Merlin says I need a plan to defeat the wizard. Maybe you can help, since you go on a lot of quests," I told Bralyn. "Have you ever had to defeat a much more powerful enemy?"

"Not one who didn't know I was coming. It is dishonorable to attack an unaware opponent. However, that really only pertains to non-magic users. In this case, catching him by surprise is your best weapon. Well, that and your staff."

"My staff is unreliable. Merlin, how were you defeated?"

*"I was distracted and captured in the syrus."*

"Then we can do that to the wizard."

"Do what?" Bralyn asked.

"I know you said you would get us there, but I don't expect you to help us fight."

"That is part of your mission as well, so of course I'll help. What's the plan?"

I considered pushing again to know why he was so determined. Furthermore, this was supposed to be my chance to prove myself. *If I have a warrior helping me fight, what would that prove?*

"*Even the most powerful sorcerer needs allies,*" Merlin said as if he heard my thoughts.

*Wait, can he hear my thoughts?*

"*Only rarely,*" he said. "*You have the ability to speak telepathically to me and I suspect you will learn to by accident.*"

"Okay, if you two can distract him, I may be able to come up with a curse that can subdue him long enough to trap him in the syrus box. Since Merlin is bigger than the box is, I'm assuming size doesn't matter."

"*What about my curse?*"

"You two can go in, pretending you're visiting him to get your curse broken. Wizards always help people who travel on a long journey to seek their help. After your curse is broken, I'll trap him."

"Do you have enough power to curse such a strong wizard?" Bralyn asked.

"I don't know. I guess it depends on timing and how well you can distract him. If he's not fighting me, I can use my staff. Hopefully, it won't do something weird. Maybe I can turn him to stone like I did the rabbits."

"*You can poison him,*" Merlin suggested.

"No way."

"You can poison him," Bralyn suggested, having not heard Merlin.

I gaped at him. "Why is that okay for you? *I'm* the sorcerer here, and I don't want to poison someone. That is too cruel even for me."

"You would rather face him so he can fight back and possibly kill you?" Bralyn asked.

"Yes… I mean no. I don't know. I don't know what I want. I just want to be a sorcerer that everyone fears." I tried to consider poisoning him, but the thought made me sick. The only poisons I knew were painful and slow. Nobody deserved to suffer in pain while knowing without a shadow of doubt that they were going to die and there was nothing they could do about it.

Bralyn continued. "I admire and approve of your decision. It will be an honor to lose with you."

Merlin groaned. *"I cannot believe this is really happening… again. How do I always end up in these situations?"*

\* \* \*

We walked in silence for a while before I heard the sound of the ocean. "Please tell me you have a boat," I said just as we reached the top of the hill that overlooked the ocean. The road led straight to a dock for huge ships.

"No, of course not. Our ride is already here."

I groaned. "You're joking, right? Please tell me we're not getting on *that*."

"No, I'm not joking."

The only ship at the dock was massive and had distinctive swords on the sail. It was a pirate ship.

# CHAPTER 9

Merlin and Bralyn strolled towards the pirate ship like it was an everyday occurrence. I was hesitant for obvious reasons. Pirates were the most ruthless scoundrels and thieves at sea. Because sorcerers typically stayed on land and pirates typically stayed on the ocean, I had never met one personally. I would have been perfectly happy to never meet one.

With a sigh, I followed.

"*Be mindful of what you say when you speak to the captain,*" Merlin advised.

"I know. If I'm too nice, he'll try to walk all over me."

"*Or he will kill you. Also, be careful not to answer me, as it looks like you are talking to yourself to those who cannot hear me.*"

"I know."

"You know what?" Bralyn asked. I shook my head. "Do you want me to seize the ship by force or coerce the pirates to take us where we want to go?"

I gaped. "Do you fight everyone? What happened to, 'We are still people'?"

"I'm a warrior. Yes, I'm also a person, but fighting is what I do."

"You said quests were what you do."

"You are seriously overthinking this. You're a sorcerer; you know how it is."

I grimaced. Sorcerers were known to work well with warriors because they both had a price and neither of them was afraid of getting their hands dirty. "I think we should try to pay them first, and you can do what you have to if they refuse."

We reached the dock then, but before we could take a step onto it, a pirate jumped down from the ship and glared. He was a heavyset man with long, tangled, greasy black hair and a beard to match. Under all that hair was a wide, dirty face with a long, crooked nose and eyes the color of sea foam. He was as large as Bralyn in both height and girth, but he had as much fat as muscle, whereas Bralyn only had muscle.

"Hello," Bralyn said brightly. "We are trying to get to the Island of Light. Would you be able to help us?"

The pirate scowled at him. "No. Go away." His voice was not as deep as I had expected; it was actually more nasally and scratchy.

"We can pay you," Bralyn insisted.

"You have nothing I want."

"We have gold," I cut in.

The pirate just sneered. "I have gold. I have three private islands full of gold. The way to the Island of Light is treacherous. Why would I risk my life and the lives of my crew?"

"Well, what do you want?"

"Food!" another pirate shouted. We looked up to see three other pirates at the edge of the ship, all listening to our conversation intently.

"You don't have food?" I asked.

"We have fish. We have all kinds of fish, and we're sick of it," the pirate in front of me growled.

"*Ask him who the captain is. Only the captain can make a deal,*" Merlin said.

"Are you the captain?" I asked the pirate. He was bigger than the others and the only one to step off the boat.

"I am. My name is Bloodbath."

"Really?" I asked, my jaw dropping. Before his scowl could turn even more venomous, I asked, "And you're sick of fish?"

"You would be sick of anything if it was all you ate for two years."

I was so sick of apples and broccoli after six days of eating them that I never wanted to see them again, so I could understand his frustration. "Great. Then I do have something you might want. Bring me one of your fish." He only stared at me. "Really, I can help. Just one fish."

He still looked skeptical as he turned to his crewmates. "Toss him a fish."

A moment later, one of the pirates tossed a little fish at me. I caught it with my free hand, but almost dropped it because it was so slimy. Once I had a firm grip on it, I pointed my staff at it clumsily. Fortunately, the fish was already dead. I couldn't transform a live animal into a dead one, which was why I couldn't conjure meat with my wand.

*Change this to meat.* The crystal on the staff glowed once again and the fish changed into the same tofu I had tried the other night.

Merlin groaned. "*You cannot give that to him; if he hates it, he might eat us.*"

Bloodbath was excited when he saw the meat, however, and took it from me. Juice seeped into his beard as he shoved half of it into his mouth and I had to force myself not to gag on his behalf. To my surprise, he ate it whole, bone and all. "I have no idea what that meat was, but it was absolutely delicious!" he declared. The other pirates cheered.

"Great! It's called tofu. Merlin said it's a great source of protein, whatever that is. So you'll take us to the Island of Light if I turn your fish into tofu?"

"You have a deal. Come aboard! Had I known a wizard could be so powerful, I would have kidnapped one long ago."

"Actually," I pointed out quietly, "I'm a sorcerer, not a wizard."

He frowned. "Really? But I thought…" He indicated his hair.

I blushed. "Yeah."

"And I thought…" He held his hand out in front of his chest in a rough estimate of my height.

I blushed deeper. "Yeah. I have a sorcerer staff, though," I said, trying to be positive. "And this is my sorcerer family's mark." I pointed out the gold emblem on my robe.

"I see," he said, obviously not convinced.

"He may look small and feeble," Bralyn cut in, "but he conjured a beast of unimaginable horrors to carry out his villainous quest."

That must have been all the confirmation Bloodbath needed because he turned to his crewmates. "Men, this is the sorcerer…"

"Ayden Dracre, and this is Merlin," I said.

"I'm Bralyn Trajir, a warrior."

Bloodbath turned back to his pirates. "This is Ayden, the great sorcerer who can change fish into food, Bralyn the warrior, and Merlin the… extinct land animal."

Merlin growled. "He's a wizard," I said quickly.

Bloodbath frowned again. "Really? You're a sorcerer… and he's a wizard? I must have been at sea for too long."

\*       \*       \*

We were soon on our way. Aside from the captain, there were five pirates on the ship. The only one who wasn't dirty, hairy, and huge was Jevwen, who was the captain's son. He was about sixteen, slender, and clean compared to the others. His hair was even short, albeit crudely cut, and his clothes were obviously sewn by himself. He had the same bone structure as his father, so he would look very similar if he put on weight and broke his nose a few times. However, he seemed to have no interest in doing that.

While the other pirates brought fish for me to transform, Jevwen sat in his bed below deck and read. I wanted to read, too, but the books were in a foreign language. The young man was clearly perfectly happy being a scholar instead of following his father's legacy of sea-pillaging. Even more astounding to me was how proud Bloodbath looked when he introduced Jevwen to me. I was glad he could be so free.

It was dark and cramped below deck with a row of ten beds narrowly spaced along the right wall and wooden crates taking up the rest of the room. Each pirate had his own box of personal stuff, except for Jevwen who had two. Other than that, the crates contained everything from writing paper to jewelry, since the pirates were pillaging different treasures from different places and ships.

Finally seeing the end in sight for this journey and finally so close to proving myself, I started to feel a little giddy. That was until Bloodbath informed me that the trip would take five days.

\*      \*      \*

On the first day, it was okay. I used my staff to create fire in an iron bowl and cooked fish for Bralyn, Merlin, and me, while the rest of the crew ate tofu. Bralyn didn't like tofu any more than I did. Many of the pirates were anxious about having a sorcerer on board, but they warmed up to me quickly. Merlin spent most of the day lying in one of the beds below. He said he was just tired, but I knew it was sea sickness.

When the sun set, sea mist made it impossible to keep a candle lit on the deck, and since it was a cloudy night, the moons provided little light. I still wasn't comfortable on the ship, so I made my wand light up and sat with Jevwen. We told each other funny stories of our childhood. Mine were sad. Soon, the rest of the pirates joined in and I learned how they all came to live here with what was undoubtedly the most successful pirate I'd ever heard of.

Unlike everyone who was born with magic, non-magic users had a choice in how they wanted to live their lives. Bloodbath enjoyed the sea and hated taking commands, so he had chosen pirating based on that. Bloodbath was his pirate name, of course, and nobody knew his real name. Jevwen enjoyed traveling, so when he turned fourteen, he left his mother and found his father. Once the other pirates were out of tales, they got back to work or went to sleep, leaving me alone with Bloodbath. I told him my story, and he was quiet when I went to bed.

\*　　\*　　\*

On the second day, I woke with cramps in my shoulders and neck. There were enough beds for all of us, but I hadn't been prepared for how rocky the ship was and how loud the crashing waves could get. Merlin refused to teach me anything or even let me use my staff to practice for the upcoming battle, saying he remembered how easy it was for these types of ships to sink.

I didn't want him to tell me how easy it was.

\*　　\*　　\*

I was awoken on the third day with the tip of a sword at my throat. Only the sparse moonlight streaming in through one of the hatches reached my bed, but it was enough to identify the man threatening my life.

Sorcerers were masters of magic, yet that didn't help me at all when Dessa had a dagger to my back or when there was a sword to my throat. I glanced at Merlin's bed, but he wasn't in it. When the blade was finally retracted, I was able to breathe again.

"Why?" I asked.

"You are about to face an enemy of unimaginable power, but I could have easily killed you in your sleep just now. You need to hone your survival instincts," Bloodbath said, harnessing his sword. "Have you ever been taught to use a sword?"

"My father tried to, but I was so bad at it that it wasn't worth the risk. I was little at the time, though."

"Come up to the deck and I will start training you with the sword. You won't master it before you face Magnus, but even a little training is better than none."

I followed him reluctantly up the stairs and groaned when I saw that it wasn't even daylight yet. Before I could retreat back down the steps, Bloodbath handed me a sword.

"Face me." He showed me how to stand, how to swing, and how to block. "Only in enactments, lovers' spats, and entertainment do they clash blades intentionally," he said. "When the blades strike, it dulls them, but it is better to dull your blade than lose your leg or worse. Against another person, you don't need as much force as you probably think you do. A person's body is not that strong. If you are fighting a monster, however, put as much force in it as you can, because too much is better than not enough."

"I can't hold my staff and a sword at the same time."

"That is true, but you have already told me that your staff doesn't always do what you want it to. A sword only does what you make it; any failure is on you. If the hilt breaks, that is still your fault. Someday, a sword may save your life where magic lets you down."

I practiced all day. Merlin watched and Bralyn took over teaching me several times when Bloodbath wanted a break. By the end of the day, I could barely hold the sword at all and I couldn't feel my hands. Bloodbath gave me a drink from a large brown bottle, told me it would help me feel better, and then just laughed when I asked him if it was a healing potion. It definitely wasn't a potion; it made me feel worse for a short time... and that was the last thing I remembered.

\*     \*     \*

On the fourth day, I woke without any pain. In fact, I felt great until I went back up onto the deck and was immediately handed a sword. "Can't I eat first?" I asked.

"When you cut me, you can eat," Bloodbath answered.

I looked at Jevwen, who was watching us. He shrugged. "It was how he taught me. I went many days without food."

I turned to Merlin. "I'm hungry."

The wolf smirked. *"You wanted to be the strongest sorcerer. That requires daily practice in all kinds of skills. Trust me, I am taking notes. Apparently, I was not hard enough on you."*

I hoped that he was joking.

\*     \*     \*

The sun was getting low in the sky and there didn't appear to be an end in sight for my training when we heard a shout from Jevwen. He pointed to something in the distance, but it was too far for me to make out. "There's a bad storm out that way."

"That's the way to the Island of Light, though, isn't it?" I asked.

"It is," Bloodbath said, harnessing his sword and joining Jevwen. "Can you tell how it's moving?"

Jevwen held up a slender metal object to his eye and looked at the storm through it. "No, not yet."

"Keep an eye on it." He then addressed the other pirates and told them to lower the sails and close the hatches to the cargo. When he checked back with Jevwen, the boy didn't have good news.

"It's coming right for us, and it's coming fast."

"You and Ayden need to get below."

Jevwen nodded, but helped his father lower the sail instead. I helped close the holes into the lower deck until thick clouds blocked out the sun. By then, the waves and wind were getting violent. Finally, Jevwen, Merlin, and I went downstairs. Bralyn insisted on staying and helping in any way he could.

Merlin settled on the bed and rested his head on his paws.

"It'll be okay," I told him.

"*I know, but that storm was not normal and I have a very bad feeling about this.*"

"There was something odd about the storm," Jevwen said as he started pulling down books from his shelf. For a while, he was wrapped up in that. The ship continued to rock violently until even I felt sick. "Here!" Jevwen shouted, causing me to jerk in surprise. He shoved his book into my hand and pointed to a bunch of foreign words.

"I can't read that."

"It's a Charybdis; a sea monster. I knew that storm wasn't natural. A Charybdis is causing it." He turned the page and I saw a drawing of the monster.

Merlin sat up. *"Then we have a very big problem."*

It looked like a fat worm that was widest at its mouth and gradually narrowed into a thick spiked club on its tail. Its mouth was actually its entire head. It was drawn with its mouth open wide and, if the drawing was accurate, it wasn't a mouth that was designed to close.

The creature appeared to have both scales and fur, like it couldn't decide if it wanted to be a dragon or a mammal. It also had two flippers close to its head, but the flippers had claws, like a sea turtle's.

"Please tell me you're not sure about this."

"I am. I've heard stories of it before. Trust me; this is the Charybdis."

"Okay, so we should be fine then. Monsters don't eat ships, right?"

*"Only if there are people on them,"* Merlin said. *"Ask him if his book says how to defeat a Charybdis."*

I did, and Jevwen shook his head. "Nobody has ever defeated one. In fact, no one has ever faced one and lived to tell about it. It'll swallow our ship whole."

"Then I don't see a choice. I'll have to stop it with magic."

"This is a legendary *sea* monster," Jevwen argued. "Sea monsters are bigger and more dangerous than anything you will ever face on land."

"Not while my mother is still alive. I understand that we have no chance, so please; point out another option that I'm missing. I'm all for it."

He didn't have an answer.

I went back upstairs, ignoring their protests, and was immediately soaked by huge waves that were crashing over the deck of the ship. Although the sky was dark with furious clouds and the wind was violent, it wasn't raining, which was just further proof that this wasn't a normal storm.

I pulled my wand out of my pocket with my right hand, pointed it towards the center of the storm, and held my staff in front of me with my left hand like a shield. It quickly became obvious that the boat was circling the heart of the storm. Furthermore, it was increasing in speed.

When I looked over the edge of the boat, I realized how much trouble we were really in. A whirlpool had opened up in the sea and it was growing in size. Inside the vortex, I saw row after row of long, sharp teeth. It was the mouth of a creature that could easily swallow the ship and everyone on it. And we were circling closer and closer into it.

With panic and desperation, I used both the wand and staff at the same time. The only command I gave them was to save everyone on the ship. Red and white magic met in the middle, formed bright blue lightning, and shot into the mouth of the Charybdis. At first, I thought the magic had no effect, but then the vortex stopped growing and began shrinking.

There was no moment of relief, because I knew it wouldn't be that simple. I felt something bash against the other side of the boat— something strong enough to send the large pirate ship spiraling out of control. Well, more out of control than it had already been.

I realized what had struck the ship when a massive tentacle, easily the size of an ancient tree, reached out of the ocean and came down. Apparently the Charybdis wasn't the only sea monster hungry this night. Either that or the drawing hadn't done the Charybdis justice.

Something in me seemed to snap, and suddenly my wand and staff were just extensions of my magic. Energy stirred inside of me, swelled, and burst outward before I even realized what I was seeing. Calmness was all that was left in me as blue light engulfed the entire ship. All I could think was that we would live. We would live because I said so.

When the light faded, we were alive. We were away from the monsters.

We were stranded on land in the middle of some tropical island.

# CHAPTER 10

"What did you do?" one of the pirates, Lasender, asked me angrily.

I was too busy having no clue to answer him. Unfortunately, Lasender tried to grab me, undoubtedly to shake me. Merlin latched onto his arm before he could touch me and he shouted in pain when Merlin tossed him to the ground. When he scrambled backwards to get away, Merlin didn't go after him.

"He saved our lives," Jevwen said, exiting the lower deck.

"How do you know? You were below!" Lasender said.

"Never talk to my son like that!" Bloodbath demanded, putting his hand on Jevwen's shoulder in a show of support. "I saw that Ayden single-handedly fought the monster and transported us to somewhere safe."

"Safe or stranded?" Lasender inquired.

"We have lost ships before. We will survive this and that's thanks to Ayden."

"I'm not really sure what I did," I said. Merlin studied the crystal in my staff, which was now almost completely clear with just the slightest red coloration in the center. I didn't think that was a good thing.

*"This is a very good thing."*

"How is it good? It doesn't even look like a sorcerer's staff anymore."

*"It is more powerful than ever. It has bonded with your power and is now your staff as much as the wand is."*

"But I need dark magic to be a sorcerer."

*"You need dark intentions to be a sorcerer. The magic will do what is in your heart, so if you desire it enough, you can do dark magic. The staff still has its own personality, though."*

"Well, that's... bothersome."

"What are you talking about?" Bloodbath asked.

"Sorry, I'm just talking to Merlin."

"Oh. You really need to figure out how to not do that. You sound a little insane."

"I want a wolf to teach me to be a sorcerer," Jevwen said. Everyone looked at him and his eyes widened dramatically. "I never wanted to be a pirate." He slapped his hands over his mouth as if he hadn't meant to say that.

"I suspected as much," Bloodbath said.

"I'm sorry. I never wanted to disappoint you."

"That's why he never told you what he was doing when he went off on his own once a year at the---" one of the pirates started.

"You promised not to tell him that!" Jevwen screeched, interrupting him.

The pirate blushed furiously. "I don't know why I said that."

I held up my staff as if it would get their attention. "I don't think this is the time for---"

"I was really hoping Jevwen never became the next captain, because I didn't want to have to kill him to take my rightful place," one of the other pirates interrupted.

"What?!" Bloodbath asked, drawing his sword and aiming it at his crewmate.

"*They must be in shock,*" Merlin said. "*Shock can make people act unusual.*"

"Yeah, that must be it."

"It's really upsetting to know you two are talking behind our backs," Bralyn said, then slapped his hand over his mouth like Jevwen had.

*I think something's going on. Please don't be my fault.*

"*This is most definitely not your fault,*" Merlin said, obviously having heard my thoughts again.

"I think we should build a fire," Bloodbath said.

It was pretty dark as neither of our moons was full. "I don't know. My mother always said that a fire in the dark is the fastest way to give away your location. We don't know anything about this land or what it might be inhabited by."

"I'm afraid of the dark," Bloodbath said quickly, then slapped his hand over his mouth like the others. Everyone stared at him with wide eyes.

"That clears up so much," his son said.

"Something is definitely wrong. I didn't mean to say that. It's true, but I didn't mean to say that."

"*Seal their mouths. This must be some kind of truth spell,*" Merlin said.

I shuddered at the thought. "Merlin thinks it's a truth spell."

"If we're under a truth spell, then I would tell you that I didn't join you just because you took my mission," Bralyn said. "Oh, no." His face paled.

"I already knew you were lying about that." Before I could say anything else, my skin crawled. "I think we're being watched."

Merlin sniffed the air. "*I believe we are surrounded.*"

"But we haven't started a fire, so how did they find us?"

"*Maybe they spotted the massive ship that appeared in the middle of their island.*"

"We should be fine, though; we're on a ship." I looked over the edge and saw nothing suspicious, and the tropical trees weren't thick enough to hide people. "Maybe I can use magic to get the ship back into water before something bad happens." At that moment, I heard a small bang and a glob of green goo splattered across my entire front, including my chest, hands, wand, and staff. "Yuck! What is this?" I asked, dropping the staff and wand to try to wipe the slime off. Instead of coming off, however, it hardened. A moment later, my arms were stuck across my chest.

Other shots rang out and soon the entire crew was stuck in various positions around the ship. Merlin was the only one able to dodge the globs. Then arrows with ropes tied on them flew over the edge of the deck and bit into the wood. A moment later, the ship was flooded with small men. By flooded, I mean there were seven of them.

"Get off my ship!" Bloodbath demanded.

The men only came up to my abdomen, but they were built sturdy and covered in thick furs and wool hats as if they were used to a cold climate. I was sweating just thinking about it. They had, of all things, pickaxes that they grasped like weapons. From the dirt caking their bodies and the raggedy clothes they wore, I assumed they worked underground.

One of them pointed his axe at Bloodbath's throat and said in a harsh tone, "Silent be pirate death make you will."

Every pirate stopped struggling and turned their heads to stare at him in confusion. "What?" Bloodbath asked.

When another stranger tried to advance on me, Merlin growled at him and stepped in front of me. The man aimed his pickaxe, but Merlin didn't look afraid. *"Can you reach your staff?"* he asked, his tone completely calm. Although irritation could carry over, I wasn't sure I would hear worry through the mental link.

"No, and I couldn't even grab it if I could."

Two of the men picked up one of the pirates and tossed him over the side of the ship. In moments they got everyone but Bloodbath, Bralyn, Merlin, and me. Three of the men were trying to do the same to me, but Merlin was standing in their way like only a huge and carnivorous beast could. Unfortunately, my wand and staff were kicked further away during the struggle.

One of the men managed to tie a rope around Merlin's snout and two more were able to wrestle him down. A fourth man grabbed me to try to throw me over. Working hands or not, I was used to fighting for my life. I elbowed him in the nose and kicked out his knee, then winced when he collapsed, howling in pain. "Sorry," I whispered, hoping Merlin didn't hear me apologize to the enemy.

A fifth man came at me with a knife, and that was when I heard the last sound I ever would have expected on a pirate ship; a bear roared. Everyone froze with shock right before a huge brown bear threw himself in front of me and struck the small man with his massive paw. Obviously, the man was tossed right off the ship.

"You're the bear that fought the monster!" I shouted. Of course, he looked like any other bear, but there was something oddly familiar about him. At that point, I saw the green residue on his fur as if he had been bound by the goo and had broken it. I also noticed the absence of Bralyn. "You're a werebear?!"

As if to confirm my accusation, he sneezed all over the three men who were trying to subdue him.

"You're a werebear who's allergic to fur?"

One of the men used Bralyn's allergy to his advantage and buried his axe in the bear's arm. Bralyn roared again and clawed the small man across the chest, but the axe remained lodged in his flesh.

"Stop!" I shouted. For some reason, everyone did. "We don't even know who you people are or why you're attacking us. If you can't tell, we aren't here intentionally. We didn't come to invade or attack you!"

*"This is the perfect time to prove you are a sorcerer,"* Merlin said.

"I don't have my wand or staff."

*"The magic is inside of you. Think of the curse of stone you placed on those rabbits. Remember your exact thoughts and feelings, as if you had your staff in hand."*

"But I didn't think of turning them to stone; I just wanted to stop them from attacking. Besides, I can't turn *people* into stone, because I don't know if it would permanently hurt them."

*"A sorcerer would do it."*

"I know!" I yelled, angrier with myself than upset with him. I knew what I should do— what my mother would demand I do.

For my entire life, I thought I *couldn't* do dark magic. Suddenly, I knew I could. My problem wasn't my magic but my conscience. I wanted to make my family proud. It was all I ever wanted... but I didn't want to be like them. They hurt people and enjoyed it. They always won the day, they always got their way, and people respected them. Nobody respected me, not even strangers. I was a failed sorcerer, and apparently, I couldn't even help my friends because I didn't want to turn my enemy to stone.

*"If you cannot curse someone who is attacking you, there is no way you can fight Magnus."*

"Magnus is a wizard who can fight back. Merlin, do you believe I'm capable of being a sorcerer?"

Before he could answer, one of the small men asked, "Speak you remain foolish?"

"What? That doesn't even make... oh... I'm talking to Merlin. You can't hear him because he talks in my head, but I'm not talking to myself."

*"You understood that?"* Merlin asked incredulously. The stranger's eyes widened as well.

"It's a simple scramble spell. They do it at some of the seer tournaments to keep the oracles from sharing ideas. It changes the order of words and often the words into synonyms. In fact, my mother has used it sometimes to keep people from telling her secrets if she can't kill them outright for some reason. It can be activated by someone trying to tell a secret or it can be on all the time. If you let me get my wand, I can help."

The man with his axe to Bloodbath's throat turned to me. "Much us! But we having opportunity speak my entire mind to survive."

"Ah, I see. How did this happen in the first place?" Now everyone, including the strangers, was gaping at me. "He said that they are better off this way because they can't stand telling the truth constantly. I bet they can't even understand each other."

Distracted, the men let Merlin go. "Who are we at the course and a female version brought prevent house for a queen, and we went, you curse is to say, Arcana not."

"They invited a woman into their home who was on the run from an evil queen and when she left, she cursed them to prevent them from telling her secret," I translated. "So, then the truth curse was already here?"

"I saw a woman, not now to this cursed country queen of the good news that they had, but with anti-chain of the curse is not able to see. Been we have years for waiting, leaving the ship, but the cries every visit. Exstructus not only use the army to escape."

"Okay, this one is a little confusing. The queen wanted to make sure someone would tell her if they saw the woman, so she cursed the lands, but when the anti-curse was released, it didn't reach this island. They've waited for many years for a ship, but everyone who visited left screaming. The only thing they could do was build weapons to use to escape."

*"Can you break the curse?"*

"I don't know. Breaking my brothers' curses is one thing. I don't know this queen. I can easily break the scrambling spell, but that probably wouldn't be a good idea."

Bralyn sneezed again. Since the small men were too shocked over me understanding them to fight, he turned and clawed the green stuff that was holding me captive. It shattered and fell off of me easily. In turn, I gently pried the pickaxe out of Bralyn's arm.

He shifted back. "You really make me paranoid when you do that."

"Me, too," Bloodbath added.

Bralyn moved to grab my staff and wand while Merlin stood between the men and me. When Bralyn handed my tools to me, I sucked in a deep breath of relief. My first thought was that I should punish the small men by restraining them and throwing them off the boat. However, before I could even let the plan form, any anger I might have had for them faded. They hadn't hurt me, my friends, or any of the pirates as far as I knew… except for Bralyn, and he didn't even seem bothered by his wounded arm. I sensed desperation in the strangers.

"Alright, listen. I'm a sorcerer who transported the ship here and I can transport you to the bottom of the ocean. If you release all the pirates and stop attacking, however, I can help you all. It's not like the ship is overcrowded."

"You want them to come with us after they did this?" Bloodbath asked me in disbelief. Of course, he was still restrained.

"Either we bring them with us or I can try to break the truth spell."

"*Or you can curse them and be done with it, as a sorcerer would.*"

"I know, Merlin, but it's even worse knowing they are just trying to escape, like us."

He sighed. *"Like I said before; I agreed to teach you* how *to be a sorcerer, not force your hand to make you one. If you want to be a sorcerer, then curse them because they got in your way. If you want to be a decent person, then explain the mutually beneficial plan I know you have already thought up."*

"What do you think I should do?"

*"I think you should follow your heart and stop labeling yourself."*

"Release the pirates and we will be happy to help you," I said. "If we work together, we can get this ship out of here and the curses broken."

The small men all looked at each other, unsure. Finally, one of them said, "If you do not love to leave us here, so we agree with their treatment."

"Great! Then let's do this. Do you want to leave the island on the ship or do you want the curse broken?"

"Have valuable if many island resources."

"Right. Then I will get to work breaking your curse as soon as you let the pirates go." All but one of the men climbed down their ropes and started hacking at the green substance while the remaining man released Bloodbath.

"Tell your men to be gentle with my son," the captain snarled at him. "If he gets so much as a scratch, I'll break your arms off and tie you to the sail."

I didn't worry about them getting along. As far as I was concerned, this whole encounter was going well. Yes, I had stranded us on an island, but I saved us from the Charybdis. Yes, I turned down an excellent chance to prove that I was a sorcerer, but I possibly made seven new allies. And most importantly, I was on an island with a truth spell over it and I hadn't blurted out anything embarrassing.

"*Why did you not tell me about the bear?*" Merlin asked.

"Um… it slipped my mind."

"*Really?*"

"No, of course not. I lied. I'm a liar. I'm lying. Get over it." Everyone stared at me. "Sorry, just something I lied to Merlin about."

"*You lied when you said it slipped your mind?*"

"Yes, I just said that."

"*Then you just now lied.*"

"So?" I asked. He gave me a look until I suddenly got it. "Oh. I am the most powerful and evil sorcerer and I cause pain and destruction as often as possible." I paused, waiting for some backlash or compulsion. "That's odd. How come I can lie?"

The small man's face was ashen, as he obviously thought I was telling the truth.

"You couldn't be evil if you were enchanted by a sorcerer to have all your kindness removed," Bloodbath said.

That hurt. "There's no reason to be mean!"

He grimaced. "I don't think it's a bad thing. Any sorcerer I've ever heard of would have tried to kill me and take my ship. You bargained. Many people see weakness and kindness as the same thing and will try to walk all over you."

I pushed aside those negative thoughts. To end this truth spell, I had to find the weakness in it. Fortunately, I already had a clue; it wasn't working on me. "Merlin, can you lie right now?"

"*No.*"

"Then it's not magic that's keeping me safe from the compulsion spell. Everyone, leave me alone for a while so that I can think." I climbed down the rope and then walked away. Once I was out of sight of the boat, I sat down and leaned against a tree. My staff and wand felt so right in my hands, but this was a deeper curse than I was used to dealing with, so I had to focus.

I let the quiet peace of my surroundings seep into my mind and my magic seep into the world around me. There was dark magic and white magic, but magic was magic and I was still highly trained in it, even if I was terrible at using it to cause mayhem. I felt my magic encounter the natural forces of the world peacefully. In fact, the only conflict I sensed was between my wand and staff.

*There's the weak point.* I could feel it. The spell was created out of hate and paranoia. The person who cast the spell did so with almost no structure. She may have been powerful, but as far as being a sorceress went, she was an idiot. For one thing, someone could avoid spilling their secrets by simply not thinking about it. If they thought of a secret, however, they had to tell it.

In this very unusual case, the weakness was that the caster was reacting with hate and fear. My mother always told us that the fastest way to fail was to fear failure, and that was exactly what the caster did.

I had only ever heard of a spell like this; it was a spell that a person could break with love.

Why I was immune to it, I didn't know. It wasn't because I was more powerful than the person. There were several ways to come at breaking the curse, but none were as simple as using the caster's weakness against her.

Merlin joined me then. "*I know you wanted privacy, but I thought now would be a good time to step in. You have figured out what it takes to break the spell, correct?*"

"Yes. There are several ways, but---"

"*But love and loyalty is the spell's weakness,*" he interrupted.

"How did you know that?"

"*I may be trapped in this form and without magic at the moment, but I am still a wizard. Am I correct in assuming you have never loved a woman before?*"

"Are you joking? The first girl I knew sneered at me because I refused to give her a poison for her tutor. Women who date sorcerers want strong, violent, dangerous men like my brothers. They don't want someone with compassion. Women who want love and compassion wouldn't look twice at me because of my family."

"*Believe it or not, I understand. Although I have no magic right now, I can at least break this curse.*"

"But you might betray someone you loved."

"*I will not. Had you cursed those strangers, as a sorcerer would have, we would not be here and I could have kept my secret.*"

"I'm sorry. I just wanted the fighting to stop and I didn't want to hurt the strangers."

"*If you had, I would not be telling you this. I was a stranger to everyone. I traveled the worlds and never looked back. In my younger years, I was compulsive and made a lot of mistakes because I wanted to help everyone, but I also had too much pride. I thought my abilities made me better than other people. When these mistakes blew up in my face, I made excuses. And then, I met an enemy greater than myself. He was wise, powerful, and truly ruthless. The second greatest mistake of my life was challenging him, and it was also the best thing for me. He made me ageless and trapped me in a crystal cave.*

"*When I finally escaped, I was not the same man. Hundreds of years had passed and the worlds had changed. Before the cave, I believed I had everything. By the time I escaped, I realized I had nothing. Worldly treasures were nothing to a lonely man. For hundreds of years, I was missing, and nobody knew. Nobody missed me. For hundreds of years, I had nothing but time to reflect on the mistakes I had made. When I looked upon the new world, I vowed to never regret. Before acting, I would consider the mark I would leave on the world."*

"So it made you wise?"

*"It did. I was even an advisor to young wizards and kings. However, as old as I was, I still had a lot of learning ahead of me. There were women I loved, but when they discovered that I would never age, none of them thought I was worth it, or they believed they could use me."*

"Use you how?"

*"Use me to attain immortality. Then I met a young woman named Nimue. She was not rich or powerful, but she was pure of heart. I cannot say why she ever loved me back. She left her family to travel with me and asked that I teach her magic. It was the happiest time in my long life."*

"What happened?"

*"Another wizard set his eyes on her. When he failed to sway her, he cursed her so that anyone she felt love for would change into a beast."*

"And he sealed you?"

*"No."*

"Then what happened?"

*"That is a secret I will keep to myself, which is why I just broke the truth spell."*

I blinked, remembering why we were out here in the first place. "I don't understand."

*"I know. Just know that Nimue is the reason I am still here today, and I will never betray her secrets. No spell can make me do so, which is how I broke this one."*

"So if I asked you what the seer told you, you wouldn't be compelled to answer?"

"*I would have had to answer had you asked me ten minutes ago.*"

I took that to mean he wasn't going to tell me. "Do you want me to try to break your curse?"

"*Not tonight.*"

"Do you think I could do it? You can lie to me if you want to make me feel better."

He smirked. "*I know you could break it. Now, we should get back to the others before the pirates and dwarfs start fighting.*"

# CHAPTER 11

We returned to the dwarfs and pirates, who were in fact, arguing. It was very inefficient arguing, too, because the pirates couldn't understand the dwarfs. I waved my wand at them. *Break the scramble spell*, I thought to the wand. Such spells were child's play for my wand. Unfortunately, the glittery white magic that was produced bounced joyously into the pirates and dwarfs alike. "Don't you start acting like the staff," I told my wand.

Too late, though. The wand's magic broke the scramble spell, but it also cleaned the men up. They were now all washed, clean-shaven, and their clothes were hole-free. Needless to say, they were not happy. Better smelling, yes, but not happy at all.

"What did you do that for?!" Bloodbath asked, rubbing his short, clean, brushed hair as if his tangled mess was hiding underneath it.

"Sorry," I said. Merlin made a growling sound of disapproval and I sighed. "I mean I'm not sorry because I'm a sorcerer and I have no sympathy or mercy."

"A sorcerer with blond hair and blue eyes?" one of the dwarfs asked skeptically.

"I understood that!" another exclaimed happily. He then sniffed his shirt and gagged. "I think I preferred the scramble spell. I smell like a woman now; all clean and proper. I'm going to go and roll around in the mud." All of the pirates and dwarfs except for Jevwen were in agreement and headed off somewhere to dirty themselves.

"*Wow*," Merlin said. "*You ended their fighting with just one little spell.*"

"I didn't mean to."

"The truth spell must be over," Jevwen said.

"Try to move the ship," Bralyn suggested.

"It might be a better idea to do that with us on it, in case I transport it too far away. Besides, it has been a very long day and I need a nap."

"*Speaking of which, I could do with some food.*"

So Merlin ran off to hunt while Jevwen and Bralyn gathered wood for a fire. It was my intention to start a fire with magic when they returned, but I fell asleep before they did.

*       *       *

I woke to the sound of manual labor, which immediately made me want to find a hole to hide in. Two things I always avoided were my brothers and hard work. I opened my eyes and saw Merlin sitting next to a dying fire.

With his snout, he indicated a crudely shaped ceramic plate beside him with roasted meat on it. "*Eat.*"

I did. It was very different from tofu and I was very hungry, so I devoured it like I hadn't eaten in days. The sound of work was actually the pirates and dwarfs trying to move the ship on their own. I knew they couldn't budge it, but it seemed to make them feel better to try.

"*Are you ready to finish this?*" Merlin asked.

I nodded, still watching them. "I don't know if I can do it, though. You were right last night; there's no way I can defeat Magnus when I couldn't even curse the dwarfs. Maybe I should give up."

"*Give up and do what?*"

I shrugged. "Go back home and hope my mother is quick about it."

"*Knowing your mother would kill you, why would you go back home?*"

"She wouldn't let me be free. I think the only reason she hasn't sent something to hunt me down and kill me yet is because if my brothers are killed fighting Magnus, then I'm the only one left. I don't know why she hasn't killed me before."

"*I suspect it is because you are the seventh son. You are useful to her.*"

I disagreed, but I didn't feel like talking about it. Fortunately, I didn't have to, because Bralyn joined us. "Are you going to lend a hand or let these men continue to humiliate themselves all day?" He then sneezed and had to move further away from Merlin.

I rolled my eyes, grabbed my staff and wand, and stood. I imagined the ship lifting until it was hovering just off the ground. Magic raced through my body and out of the wand and staff. Like before, the magic merged into some beautiful blue energy that surrounded the ship and lifted it, just as I had imagined.

*"It is interesting how neither your wand nor staff does exactly as you say, but together, they respond flawlessly. Did you notice that?"* Merlin asked.

I nodded. Although the magic required to levitate an object was pretty simple, the force required to lift something so massive was taxing. For the pirates and dwarfs, it was suddenly weightless, so they began pushing it easily. I was out of breath before I could even see the beach, but I persisted. The energy grew darker blue every passing moment until my vision started becoming dark and a stabbing headache formed.

Then, just when the ship started to falter, I felt new energy. Merlin was giving me his strength through the weird psychic connection we had. It felt like much of the pressure was off of me, so I was able to hold it up for that last thrust the pirates and dwarfs needed. Soon, they couldn't push it any further, so the pirates climbed up the ropes and I let the water guide it to the drop-off. When it was finally far enough in the water, I let it go.

"Great, now how do we get in?" Bralyn asked.

"We swim."

*"I will not,"* Merlin said.

"Fine." I waved my wand upward before either of them could argue. White, glittery magic surrounded us in an obscenely pretty fashion, and then we were on the ship. Bralyn gasped with horror and tried to brush off the excess glitter from his clothes and skin. "Yeah, it does that. Sorry." Merlin was even more horrified, and it was completely called for.

For some reason that I could not fathom, the wand thought he needed a pretty pink bow around his head. There was death in his eyes as he gave me a glare that I was sure even my mother felt. I carefully tugged on one end of the ribbon until the bow came loose and then tried to brush the glitter away from his face.

"So, good news and bad news," Bloodbath said. "The good news is that we found out from the dwarfs where we are. The bad news is that we are now two days away from the Island of Light."

"Please tell me you're joking."

Jevwen handed him two wooden swords. "And look what we found safe below deck."

\*     \*     \*

We were approaching the island from the other side this time, so we hoped we wouldn't have to deal with another monster. At about sunset, I went below deck to ask Jevwen if he had any books on the Island of Light, only to stop at the bottom of the steps. Behind some of the crates were Jevwen and Bloodbath arguing about the teen's future. Jevwen wanted to learn magic, but he didn't think he had any abilities. Bloodbath wanted his son to pursue that dream, but he was afraid that it was too dangerous.

I returned to the upper deck and found everyone stuffing their mouths with the fruit that the dwarfs gave them. It was odd to me that a pirate could be so concerning about his son, since I always thought of pirates as magic-less sorcerers of the sea, but I never knew sorcerers to care about their children like that. It was almost as if my family was the exception.

Merlin sat beside me. "You're not going to eat fruit?" I asked.

He shook his head. "*I am a wolf.*"

"Well, you weren't always one."

"*Correct. Before I was cursed, I lived quite happily on vegetation, fruit, and grain. I always felt that it made me a better wizard to deny myself flesh. However, the mere thought of anything other than meat makes me feel ill now. If I had no choice, I could sustain myself on other food temporarily.*"

"Oh. I can live on anything as long as it's not every day. Or tofu. I don't think I could live on tofu."

The next morning, I used the ink Merlin got at the seer tournament to color my hair black. Bralyn and the pirates thought it looked great, but Merlin said it didn't suit me.

\* \* \*

When I saw the island in the distance, I felt less prepared than ever. I had the box, magic, and sort of a plan, but a huge part of me doubted if this was the right thing to do. There would be no going back from this. If I defeated Magnus, my family would have no choice but to respect me and I would never be a disappointment to them again. *But would I ever be able to sleep at night knowing that I attacked someone like this? What choice do I have?* I was born to be a sorcerer. Sorcerers always prevailed. They were respected.

If I fought Magnus and failed, if I was killed, at least my mother would believe I wasn't a coward. To die at the wizard's hands or my mother's… *Magnus would be merciful and make it quick. That's what wizards do.* I wondered if Merlin ever felt torn between being a wizard and acting on selfish desires. I wondered if he ever wished he could be a sorcerer, because then it wouldn't be so wrong to wish that I had a choice.

If I were born of a lesser-known family, a magic-less family, or any family at all that wasn't in sorcery or wizardry, I would have a choice.

*"Is your family's respect for you worth more than your own self-respect?"* Merlin asked as he joined me.

I hadn't realized I was standing at the edge of the deck, watching the island for a long time. "This isn't supposed to bother me. Everything about sorcery makes sense to me. I just don't know why I don't want to be like my brothers. I would rather read books and create potions that make everything taste like sweet berries than steal and create poisons. I wouldn't mind having lots of money and… and all that other stuff that we get, but why? We have magic. We can trade things and do favors and yes, we may get stuck with bad deals. Sorcerers never allow themselves to be taken advantage of, but I've been traveling with you for days and we haven't needed money or been wronged. It's dangerous sometimes, sure, but it's so much more fun than…"

*"More fun than what?"* he asked eventually.

"My life has always been about trying to match my brothers. This is so much more fun than hiding in my room or cooking potions. I've made friends. Nobody liked me before because I was such a failure as a sorcerer."

*"I do not believe you ever needed me to teach you to be a sorcerer. You obviously have the power and you know what choices a sorcerer*

*would make. I think you just wanted someone who would believe in you long enough for you to start believing in yourself. So tell me what you want to do."*

I stared at the island for a moment. "We'll go in, meet the wizard, and see if he can remove your curse. If he can't, we'll trap him in the box and bring him to my mother. If he can, we'll trap him in the box and not bring him to her, until I can come up with something else." It was silent for a moment as I thought of all the magic I did since beginning this mission and how my magic never did anything actually harmful to anyone. Then I laughed. "I made a bunch of swords into flowers."

*"You made the captain of a pirate ship, all his men, and seven dwarfs* smell *like flowers."*

We both laughed for way too long, until it slowly faded into an awkward silence. We got closer and closer to the island. It was not a large island by any means; it was only large enough for the castle and a small collection of trees around it. The castle was beautiful, tall, and white as the purest magic, with slender towers and large balconies that overlooked the sea.

Sorcerers were supposed to be the caste that had it all, yet our family lived in a little cabin in the woods. *Maybe it isn't so bad for wizards after all.* "Stop here," I said to Bloodbath. "It's best you don't get too close because we don't know what Magnus would do if a pirate ship got too close to his land. I'll transport Bralyn, Merlin, and myself to the island." I turned to Bralyn. "That is, if you're sure you want to do this."

He shrugged. "You saved my life. It is my honor to fight alongside you, or die as it might be in this case."

I really appreciated his confidence in me. "Thank you all for helping us get here," I told the pirates.

"Thank you for giving us food other than fish to eat. If you ever need a ride again, we'll be around. You can find us by magic, right?"

"Probably." I held my bag and staff in one hand and waved my wand with my other. I envisioned us appearing on the beach before the castle. Once again, sparkly, lavish magical energy surrounded us, blocking out everything, and then left us right in front of the castle. This time, fortunately, my wand hadn't seen the need to give Merlin a bow or cover us with sparkles.

"Are we going with the original plan? Merlin and I will distract him while you trap him?"

"Yes. You two try to get Merlin's curse removed. I'll wait until he either breaks the curse or refuses to."

"*Maybe we should wait to…*" Merlin began.

"Wait to what?" I asked.

He hesitated. "*Never mind. Let me take a quick run around to see where it is best to sneak in.*" He left without another word.

"What's he doing?" Bralyn asked.

"Avoiding me," I answered. We waited as he took far too much time scouting the place. I started to become seriously worried.

He finally returned. "*I cannot use magic, but I can sense it. Every door and window in the back except for the garden entrance is guarded with a ward over it. If you get too close to one of the wards, Magnus will sense you.*"

"Then I'll have to go through the garden. What kind of traps and monsters will I face?" I imagined everything from more rabid rabbits to mutated glob monsters.

*"That is what worries me; there is nothing there. It feels like a trap. There is a wooden fence around the garden, but it is unlocked. I managed to peer into the garden and there was nothing threatening, just some rose bushes and wild flowers."*

"Maybe he just isn't expecting anyone to be foolish enough to try to infiltrate his home. Besides, he's a wizard, not a sorcerer, so I wouldn't expect him to have the traps that sorcerers set. Give me a reasonable amount of time and then go in the front. I'll do my thing as long as I'm alive to do it. If nothing happens, just leave as if everything was normal."

Bralyn nodded, but Merlin still looked very worried. *"Ayden, I need to tell you what the seer told me,"* the wolf said.

I considered the sun, which was getting low in the sky. "Is it really that important? Can't it wait?"

He looked even more worried, so I left before he could argue.

I made my way through the trees, keeping a safe distance away from the castle and the stone wall around it. I knew I could get over the wall, but I had no idea what wards there were. Eventually, I reached the back of the castle and found a wooden gate. Since it was the only one I saw, I figured it was the garden gate, so I opened it. And I gaped at what I saw beyond.

It was the gate to the garden, but the garden was not as Merlin described. The "rose bushes" were huge hedges far taller than me with blood red roses and terribly sharp thorns. They were shaped in such a way that a person could get lost trying to make it through. "Of course." This was exactly what I expected of a magic-user, wizard or otherwise. I let the gate close behind me and started into the maze.

\*     \*     \*

I was exhausted, injured, and completely lost. At one point, I got so frustrated that I tried to go through the hedge. That was a mistake I would never make again. I was pretty sure I lost half my blood, because as soon as the thorns tasted it, the hedges didn't want to let me go. I had to actually fight thorny vines that wrapped themselves around my arms and waist.

Even worse was the fact that the sky was beginning to darken. I worried that Bralyn and Merlin had already given up on me and desperately wanted to call out to them. Only my fear that the hedges would answer my call instead kept my mouth shut.

Several times, I felt, heard, or even saw something move behind me, and the wind often sounded like it was carrying the conspiracies of monsters. It occurred to me that I could use my wand to make light, and *then* it occurred to me that I was a complete idiot. One of the first spells I had ever learned was a guidance spell. I pulled my wand out of my pocket, pushed magic into it, and told it to show me the way out. A sphere of white magic burst from the tip of the wand and fluttered in the air for a moment before disappearing in one direction. I chased after it.

I finally felt like I was getting somewhere, and seriously thought I was just about out of the maze… when the bright ball of light sank right through one of the hedges as if it was getting impatient. Unfortunately, I was also impatient. This time, I put my wand away and focused my magic into my staff.

The result was quite different. It was fire instead of light that burst from my staff and the hedges around me instantly blazed until it was nothing more than smoldering ashes on the ground. And I was surrounded by four men.

"*I just discovered what was bothering me so much about this place,*" Merlin suddenly said in my mind with a definite tone of panic. "*Whatever you do, you must not use dark magic!*"

*Too late.*

The four men had no weapons, but there was something very dangerous about them. All of them were slender and dressed from head to toe in black uniforms, which even covered up their faces and hair. The only skin they showed was their eyes. The cloth of the uniform appeared to be thin; even their boots conformed to their feet like gloves. Most odd was the white patches on their chests. On one of them was a heart, on another was a diamond, another had a spade, and the last had a club.

They took on a fighting stance. I wasn't a warrior; I had never been taught to fight. I was, however, a sorcerer; I had never been taught to let that stop me. If I was going down, I wasn't going to make it easy for them. These weren't small men who were just desperate to escape a curse.

As if some part of me needed to be sure, I let them make the first move. All four of them made a fancy motion with their hands and swords formed out of thin air. They were one-handed swords with curved, thin blades that glowed red. These were sorcerers specifically trained to fight.

Pulling out my wand again, I let magic flow through both my wand and staff. The magic once again combined into a cool blue light, but then, to my shock, it split back into white and red. White magic, laced with the magic of the staff, poured into me, dark magic, laced with the magic of the wand, struck my opponents like lightning. I felt the defensive magic protecting my flesh like the staff had done before, but the numb sensation was so much deeper.

The dark magic was also going very deep into my opponents. When they were all on the ground, moaning in pain, I actually felt disappointed. "That's it? You're Magnus's defense and you can be taken down by a little lightning?"

Apparently, they didn't like being taunted, because they all sort of… floated back up onto their feet, as if they were pulled by strings. It was creepy.

I struck again, only to immediately feel an uncomfortable draw on my energy. It was much more potent magic than I was used to, yet the men didn't go down this time. Instead, the magic seemed to be absorbed into their swords, which was about the worst thing that could have happened.

One of them swung his sword at me. I moved almost before I saw him and blocked the blow with my staff, then immediately regretted it; the idea that his sword would hurt my staff made me sick. I needn't have worried, because the staff crackled with the same blue energy that was protecting my skin.

I swung it upward, obviously catching him unaware, as it struck him squarely across the jaw and sent him flying backwards. The remaining three men attacked as one. The heart man and the diamond man used their swords, but I waved my wand and energy swarmed around me, somehow slowing their blades so that I could easily avoid them. At the same time, the man with the club on his chest held his sword up into the air as if it were a staff and violent red magic turned green. I had seen this exact curse before; the sinister energy was a poison.

I tried to think of what I was supposed to do to counteract it. I knew how to create it, but not how to defend against it. There wasn't enough time.

"Stop." The woman's voice was sudden and unexpected, like a cup smashing on the ground. The poison dissolved and we all turned to see who had interrupted our duel.

She could have been the embodiment of white magic. Her long, golden blond hair was partially braided, partially loose and draped over her shoulders, her blue eyes sparkled in the fading sunlight, and her long white robes dragged on the ground. She was slim, dainty, and not very tall, yet her aura was strong.

I opened my mouth to speak, only to shut it when I saw the necklace she wore. It was a multi-colored crystal with a silver object in the center of it. I recognized it from a book I once read. I had no idea what book, but I had definitely seen that crystal before.

She stood in the castle's doorway, where roses clung to the stone frame and emphasized her purity with their blood color. "Leave us," she said to the four men, who all bowed and then walked away. "Come in, Ayden. I have waited a long time for your visit."

I didn't move. "I'm here to see Magnus. A great seer, Dessa, told me that I would find the wizard here."

She gave me an oddly familiar half smirk. "She told you that what you seek is in the Island of Light. You may have thought you wanted to defeat Magnus, but what you really wanted was a choice."

"And you can give me a choice?"

"I can explain to you what your choices are."

"Who are you?"

"I am Livia Dracre, the seventh daughter of Morina Dracre."

"Morina Dracre is my grandmother. You're my aunt?!"

# CHAPTER 12

I followed Livia into the castle. The interior was not the kind of place I ever imagined a sorceress would live in. The ceilings were high and the walls were decorated with gold art and extravagant murals. All of the furniture was old, delicately crafted wood with soft-looking, colorful fabrics and accented with glass and gold vases and statues. Huge windows let in lots of sunlight.

"I don't understand," I said. "Is this some kind of disguise to fool wizards into thinking you're one of them? This isn't really your home, is it?"

She studied me for a moment. "I was about your age when I decided on my path, too. Let me guess, Ilvera wants to kill you?"

"How did you---"

"She can't," she interrupted.

We entered a small study with wall-to-wall, floor-to-ceiling bookshelves. The fireplace, door, and window were the only sections of the walls not covered in books. Two high-back, green suede chairs sat facing each other in front of it with a small, low table between them. The table was mostly made of glass with a sturdy-looking red wood frame. Livia gestured to one of the chairs. I sat, but before sitting herself, she pulled a white wand from inside her left sleeve and waved it at the table, where two cups of tea appeared.

I gaped. "You're really powerful."

She slipped her wand back into her sleeve, sat down, and took one of the cups. "We have different strengths. I can conjure anything, but I have trouble breaking even the simplest curse. From what I've seen, it is the other way around for you."

"You've been watching me?"

"Of course. You are my nephew after all. I had to be sure that my sister didn't turn you onto a dark path." She sat forward and ran her fingers over the emblem on my robe. "She must be so furious." Then she touched my hair and I sat back so that she had to let go. "You should change your hair back. This doesn't suit you."

"How did you see me?"

She retrieved her wand from her sleeve again and motioned with it to the table. The glass surface changed into a mirror. I squeaked.

"W-what... I mean... oh."

"All I have to do is say a person's name. Show me Ilvera."

A new shape took form in the mirror until I saw the top of my mother's cabin. Since I had seen it from the tree-tops, I recognized it easily.

"I can't actually see into her house because she has more magic than my mirror, but I could track your progress after you left." She motioned with her wand again and the mirror changed back into a table.

"Why were you watching me?"

"You are special. You see, I was the seventh daughter of the seventh daughter. Ilvera is my older sister; the sixth daughter. There was no end to her fury when she discovered that her younger sister was more powerful than her. She tried to kill me and take my power, but she never got the chance. Like you, I had a choice."

I laid my staff down on the table next to my untouched cup of tea. "A choice between being a sorcerer or a wizard?"

"Not quite. We were born with very special magic, which made us inherently neutral. It isn't so much that we can choose one or the other. It's more like we are both. My mother was a devious woman who tried very hard to rid me of all my kindness. I had just enough stubbornness to survive childhood. I fought and cursed my sisters rather than innocent people. Fortunately, my mother never knew the truth of what I was. *Unfortunately*, Ilvera found books on it and figured out why I was so much more powerful than her.

"When I was your age, my father took me to hide with another family. They were sorcerers, but they were not like the Dracre. I decided to be what I wanted to be. Ilvera hunted me down and tried to take my magic, but by then, my magic was all light or neutral, and she didn't want that. So she took the seventh son, your father, and decided to breed the next power source. She thought that if she had boys, you would be more malevolent."

I gaped. "So she ridiculed me, tortured me, and encouraged my brothers to do the same to make me become like them? That is the most ridiculous thing I've ever heard. If anything, I'm the way I am because I don't want to be like my brothers. I want them to respect me, but I don't want to treat others the way they do. Does this mean I'm a wizard?"

"Whether you choose to use light magic or dark magic, you will always have the choice. I never cared for the distinction between wizards and sorcerers. Unlike a sorcerer or wizard, you have the choice every single time. You chose to fight my guards. I chose to make my magic lighter by living this way. If I were to live around other people, I would be tempted to use both dark and light magic."

"I... don't understand."

"I know. Ilvera would never have explained it to you. The idea of being something between a wizard and sorcerer is against everything you were ever taught."

"*Ayden, are you okay?*" Merlin asked.

"*I don't know,*" I responded without thinking.

There was silence for a moment. "*Where are you?*"

"Where is Merlin?" I asked Livia.

"He and the warrior are being kept in another room. I knew you came here thinking that this was Magnus's home, but since I am not a seer, I didn't know what you would do when you discovered who I was. Both of your companions are safe."

"Let them go."

"Soon. We have much more to discuss. Particularly what to do about your brothers."

"What about them?"

"Sorcerers are important for the continuation of all magic on Caldaca, but your brothers are starting to become too destructive. Dessa warned me of what would happen if they are left unchecked. They would not stop at destroying Magnus. When they reach his castle, they will face a monstrous beast they could not be prepared for. If they fight it, it will kill Thaddeus, and your other brothers will take it out on all wizards."

*I bet it's a dragon. I'm going to be so mad if they try to hurt a poor dragon.* "None of my brothers can be taken out by a mere monster."

"That is what they believe as well. If you cannot stop them, war will break out between sorcerers and wizards."

"That's nothing new. There have been dozens of wars between them."

"Not like this. This war will take the lives of the most powerful magic-users on this world and eventually lead to the complete loss of magic for a hundred years."

"Impossible," I argued. She just sipped her tea. "I'm not going to kill my brothers."

"You must."

"You just said I had the choice between light and dark magic."

"You do, but here you only have the choice between a bad situation and a worse one. You must fight your brothers. If you face Magnus, there will be no one to stop them. I cannot tell you anything else, or I risk ruining everything. Come back to me after everything settles and I will teach you both light and dark magic. I wish I could help you."

"I can't beat my brothers. For one thing, there're six of them. For another, they know my weaknesses. If I defeat Magnus before them, that means I'm better than them. You can help me by telling me how to find him."

"I cannot. I chose my path many years ago and now it is your turn." She retrieved her wand again and waved it at my staff. White magic flowed from her wand to the crystal. "Your staff will now show you the way. I can transport you to the nearest land, but it is impossible to transport you to Magnus himself."

"But you *just* said you wouldn't help me."

"I am helping you find Magnus because your brothers are going after him. The only way for you to defeat them is to get ahead of them."

"Is it far? And how close to him are my brothers?"

"Your journey is as long as you make it. Your brothers are having a difficult time finding Magnus, but they're starting to use their heads."

"Wow. I bet it'll break something if they actually come up with a plan."

She grinned. "I guess that is another thing we have in common. Ilvera was my only sister who knew how to read. The rest of them were not intelligent enough to figure out why I was so powerful."

"So, Dessa sent me here to learn why I have white magic, but how does that help me? I'm still not going to be accepted by sorcerers or wizards."

"People will accept you when you accept yourself. Since you left home, how many people turned you away because you were not a cruel sorcerer or a selfless wizard?"

I shrugged. "Well, I lied to the elves by letting them think I'm a wizard. My family will never accept me unless I can get rid of the white magic."

She put her hand over her face with frustration. "Your family will never accept you no matter what you do. Acceptance is not in them. The only way you can be happy is to be yourself. Even then, you will have difficult decisions to make and you will have to do things that you hate, but you cannot be happy living as a sorcerer or wizard."

I stood. "You can't know that. You're using white magic without dark magic."

"That's because I made a mistake. I didn't have anyone to tell me what my choice was. I chose to lock away my darkness. I shouldn't have."

I sat back down. "What do you mean? You look perfectly happy."

"It's why I'm here alone." She rubbed the crystal pendant. "I was married long before you were born. My husband was a traveler, who had seen many worlds and never judged me on what I was. When our daughter was born, I knew she wasn't like us. Veronica even looked like the rest of the Dracre family; black hair, pale skin... but she had my blue eyes.

"She had only dark magic from the moment she was born. I thought I could teach her to be good. Even before she learned magic, she started torturing and slaughtering animals. When she was ten, she tried to kill me, so her father took her to another world.

"Out of shame, I locked away my darkness. Eventually, I fell in love with a very kind wizard and had another daughter, named Sonya. She had blond hair, blue eyes, and only goodness inside her. She only had light magic. Unfortunately, Veronica made it back to this world a few years later and learned about Sonya."

"What about Veronica's father?"

"I never saw him again. I think she killed him."

"I tried to find her and help her, but she wanted me dead. She had some strange ability to communicate with animals and even enchant them into following her orders. She killed Sonya."

"How did you defeat her?"

"I didn't. How could I harm my own child? I sent Veronica to a world where she couldn't use magic. After that, Sonya's father and I couldn't be together. We're still friends, though."

"I still don't understand."

"You and I were not meant to have only dark or only light magic."

"So no matter what I do, I'll never fit in. Maybe… what if I lock my light magic away like you did your dark magic?" I asked.

She groaned. "You have your mother's stubbornness. It might be possible, but the consequences will be horrible, and I will not be a part of it. You would lose everything you have now, including your friends."

"Where is Merlin?"

"I will let him go, just as long as you agree to defeat your brothers."

I stood up in anger. "You're holding him captive?!"

"Doesn't he mean more to you than your brothers?"

"That isn't even the issue right now! You said you only do light magic, yet you would capture someone to make me help you! I'm definitely not going to fight my brothers now!"

"I wish you would reconsider. I'm sorry about this." She made a dismissive gesture with her hands and two of the four men from the garden appeared behind me. Before

I could do anything, each of them took one of my arms and started dragging me towards the door.

No matter how much I struggled to break their grasps, the men were too strong.

"Stop," she said. They stopped, but they didn't let me go. "Sorry, but I can't have you escaping." She snapped her fingers and my wand shot out of my pocket into her hand.

"Give that back!" I yelled. I was ignored, though, and the men dragged me out into the hallway. As we passed many different rooms, I looked for Merlin, but I didn't see any sign of him. When we reached the end of a dim hallway, a third man appeared right in front of us. The outfits that hid their faces were creepy enough without jump-scares. I realized that he had a club on his clothes, as did one of the men restraining me, which meant there were more than four of these people. "Please let me go." They didn't say a word.

The man in front of us paused for dramatic effect before opening the door. I gaped. If this was what Livia thought of as a prison cell, I was okay with being captured for a while. The bed was wide enough for me to lie sideways on it and covered with richly colored blue blankets and pillows. There was a rosewood wardrobe to the left of the bed with gold accents. A small table to the right of the bed held a three-candle candelabrum.

Across from the bed, there was a window with its shutters closed and a bookshelf full of books. As soon as the masked men let me go, I went to the window and tried it. I was disappointed, but not surprised, to find it was sealed. Since there was no latch and the wooden frame was oddly warm, I figured it was locked by magic. All three men were gone by the time I turned around. I tried the door, but it was also locked.

"*Merlin?*" I asked, trying to speak in his mind again. Either he didn't hear me or he wasn't capable of answering. Unable to figure out another way out, I went to the bookshelf to see what I had to work with. There were a few old fairytale books, some history books, diaries, grimoires, and such, as well as a fair number of books written in foreign languages. I grabbed a couple of the history books and put them in my bag for Merlin.

I was searching the room for any way out when I heard a latch turn and the door opened. Livia stood there with a plate of bread, broccoli, and apples. "Have you reconsidered?" she asked, setting the plate down on the table beside the bed.

I gave her my best glare. "You should know that the Dracre do not take kindly to threats."

She nodded. "I can see the sorcerer in you, even if others can't. You are protective, and that's not a sorcerer trait, but I think if you were pushed beyond a certain point, you could be more devious than any of your brothers. Ilvera is probably counting on that."

"Then I'll warn you right now that you're on the right track if you mean to push me to that point."

"I'm not your enemy."

"You sure act like it," I said, gesturing to the whole room.

"I am not without faults, and I can't be sure how everything will turn out. All I know is that if you face Magnus, your brothers will win."

"Then you should be trying to reason with them instead of locking me and Merlin up."

"They don't have a choice; they will always be sorcerers and nothing more. You should get some sleep. Maybe tomorrow you will understand."

I opened my mouth to argue… and everything went dark.

*　　*　　*

My dreams were weird and basically involved getting locked away in a tower with Magnus's monster keeping me trapped. Merlin had to save me. I woke to a plate of potatoes and eggs. I was a little irritated that I had slept through my chance to escape and even more irritated that my aunt had used magic on me in the first place. My frustration wasn't because what she did was wrong, as I expected that from a sorceress, but because she had done it so easily. I wanted to be that powerful.

"*Merlin?*" I called, trying again to speak in his mind.

Again, I got no answer. I went to the door and tried the knob to find that it was still locked. I sat against the door and contemplated how to get out. My mother taught me potions and curses, but none of that could help me here. I was about to sigh with frustration when it hit me. Along with reading, my father taught me some life skills, like lock picking.

I pulled a pick out of my bag and got to work on the lock. It was the first time I had to use the skill without my father standing on the other side. Like most sorcerers in the world, he had a sink-or-swim philosophy. It probably had to do with his family's history with dragons. After being locked in a burning shed and forced to pick the lock to escape, I found this to be easy. I had the door open in moments.

I made my way back to the study where I hoped my wand and staff were. The room was unlocked and my magic tools were placed neatly on the table. It seemed like a trap, so I scrutinized the room instead of immediately grabbing them. Other than books, there was nothing interesting or useful. What was important was that the window was unlocked.

Of course, we were on the third floor, but it looked like I could climb down the side of the castle. The difficult part would be saving Merlin.

I was just about to try to contact him again when I heard a loud crash. I ran out into the hall to see that Merlin and Bralyn had escaped whatever Livia had used to keep them away. Merlin growled at me and I looked around for a place to run or hide, when I saw Livia standing right behind me. It was her that the wolf was growling at.

Then I started looking for a place to cover myself, because his snarl told me without a shadow of a doubt that there was going to be some blood splatter. I stepped out from between them.

"How did you…?" Livia started.

Merlin ignored her and spoke to me over her. "*You said you did not know if you were okay and then you stopped answering!*" His growl was thick even in his thought-speech.

"Merlin was worried sick over you," Bralyn said. "He tore right through the door."

"Why were you worried about me?" I asked.

"*Because I was.*" He stopped in front of Livia, still growling.

"Merlin, this is Livia Dracre… my aunt. She's the seventh daughter of the seventh daughter."

"*I know.*"

"You know what? Did you already know she was my aunt?" After a moment, he stopped growling and dipped his head in a nod.

"*I knew as soon as you told me who your mother was. I met Livia and her sisters when she was young, but I did not recognize the castle.*"

"But you knew why I'm this way."

"*I had an idea once you told me who your mother was and mentioned your brothers.*"

"So you knew I could never be a sorcerer? Were you just using me to get to Magnus so he could remove your curse?" When he didn't answer, I stepped back into the library and shut the door.

"What are you doing?" Bralyn called through the door. "This is not the honorable way to handle the truth. You should face your enemy and defeat them in battle until they conform to *your* truth."

"I need some time to be alone to think!" Since the latch was on the inside of this door instead of the outside, I flipped it to lock myself inside and sat down in one of the chairs. I didn't know what to think. I didn't want to think. No matter how much of a failure I was, I was still a sorcerer. My family tortured me, but Dracre was a respected name. Not being a sorcerer at all was… I didn't know what it was. Panic wasn't a reasonable behavior, but I couldn't get my heart to slow down. In fact, the harder I tried to calm myself, the faster my breathing became.

"Ayden, come out of there," Livia said.

"Go away!" I didn't care how whiny that sounded; I was angry, upset, and confused all at once. Merlin lied to me. My entire life, I thought something was wrong with me because I couldn't do dark magic. Livia, the aunt I never knew I had, told me that I was both a wizard and sorcerer because I was the seventh born, but that didn't make any sense either; I only ever screwed up on dark magic.

What it ultimately boiled down to was that nobody believed I could really be a sorcerer, not even Merlin. They kept talking about me accepting myself, but they all apparently had plans for me being a wizard. I could prove myself to be powerful, whether I was a wizard, or sorcerer, or whatever. I could make the choice for myself without their help.

I looked out the window, which faced the back of the castle. Bralyn had said that he used to swim from his land to this one, and sure enough, I spotted another island nearby. Without giving myself a chance to question my plan, I picked up my bag and staff, returned to the window, and transported myself to that other land.

# CHAPTER 13

I appeared right in the middle of town with my sorcerer robe billowing in the wind, the magic from the wand looking much less silly than usual, and... I tugged on a lock of my hair quickly and was excited to see that it was still black. *Yes! I look like a sorcerer...* I forced myself to stop grinning like a fool, because sorcerers didn't get excited.

People stared and moved away, but it was interest rather than sneers on their faces. I wasn't sure what to do. Livia said that my staff would show me the way, so I held it up. Nothing happened. I held it out towards the castle and then all the way around me as if I were trying to point to someone with it. When the crystal faced north, it pulsed with a deep orange light for a moment.

Although I had no reason to trust my aunt, especially after she locked me up, I didn't have anything to lose. I headed north, which was further into the heart of the city. I had never been to these lands and I doubted anyone here would know of my family, but everyone would recognize the signs of a sorcerer. It would have been easier if the crystal in my staff was still deep red instead of almost completely clear.

"Excuse me," an elderly woman said, reaching out for my arm as I passed.

I stopped and turned to her. "Yes?" I asked.

"Are you a wizard or a sorcerer?" She pointed to my staff.

"What do you need?"

"Six sorcerers came through here last night looking for someone. When nobody could help them, they took my magic roses."

"Magic roses?"

"Yes. They are eternal roses that contain transformation magic. You would be surprised how popular they are."

"I bet I would be. Who were they looking for?"

"They said he was a blond, blue-eyed young man with a green sorcerer robe that had a…" she trailed off, when she noticed my robes. "Just like that."

"Well, I'm not blond, so I'm obviously not who you're looking for. Can you tell me where these sorcerers went?"

"They haven't gone anywhere yet. They're at the tavern."

I could feel the blood drain from my face. "Where's the tavern?" She pointed to a building almost directly in front of me. "They're in there?"

"Yes. Can you get my roses back? I can pay you."

"I can't help you. Those sorcerers are the Dracre brothers, and they're dangerous." *So why are they after me?* I thought of what Livia said; I had a choice. I could defeat

Magnus, or I could not, but either way, I had to stop my brothers from being even worse than me.

I started to pour magic into my wand when someone crashed into me from behind, knocking me to the ground and everything out of my hands.

"Sorry! Sorry! I wasn't looking where I was going!" a boy yelled, scrambling back to his feet and pulling me back up. "Oh, gods! You're one of them!"

I saw him then. He was about sixteen, dressed in clean, plain clothes, with shaggy brown hair and hazel eyes. He was also backing away in fear, staring at the emblem on my chest. "No, no, don't worry. I'm not like them."

But he wasn't listening. "Please don't kill me!"

"I'm not going to kill you!" I picked up my staff and wand, but my bag had spilled open. As I began to gather my goods, the boy kneeled and helped me. He frowned at the fish that was wrapped in a cloth, but didn't comment. When everything was back in the bag, I held out my wand. Unfortunately, the sound of people laughing and arguing spilled out into the street before I could do anything, telling me that the door of the tavern had just opened. "Please don't be them. Please don't be my brothers," I whispered.

"You shouldn't have punched him," Thaddeus said. "He was just about to tell us where Magnus was."

"Of course I punched him!" Febarin argued. "He wouldn't give me that charm! Don't you realize what it did? It could make me see through illusions!"

"And why would you need that?"

"Because I might need to see through an illusion, obviously."

Febarin was the fourth son in my family and undoubtedly the least intelligent. He once proposed to a girl by cursing her entire family into an endless sleep, putting his sword to her heart, and saying that if she broke his heart, he would break hers. Terrified, she agreed, but Mother found her unworthy so Febarin let her go. I snuck out afterwards and broke his curse over her family. Although he could never prove it was me, I think he suspected it.

Despite the fact that he was short, like me, nobody called him a runt because he was very muscular. Well, there was a fair amount of fat on him as well. In fact, I would say there was more fat than muscle if I weren't afraid of losing my teeth for saying so. His hair was kept very short because Mikron used to pull on it when they were little. He also had an ugly scar on his right ear from a fight he got into with an ogre that owned his favorite tavern.

The ogre was a good family friend and tried to buy me from my mother when I was born. I suspected the ogre's intention was to eat me, but it was just as likely that he wanted to do something obscene, like make me clean his house or send me to get vegetables from the market.

I hid my face from my brothers. To my shock, they passed right by me. My black hair must have disguised me enough, along with the fact that they didn't see my face, but all of my brothers should have recognized the green robe. Just as I thought it, Thaddeus stopped and started to turn.

Instinctively, I held out my wand and let my magic surround me. An instant later, I appeared on a hilltop overlooking the city, which was my exact intention. "Let's see if I really have a choice."

I stuck my wand back into my pocket and took my staff in both hands. I imagined a bubble around the city—not one that would cut off the air, but one that would prevent anyone from entering or exiting the city. My brothers were very powerful, so I had to make it strong. Magic tingled along my skin as I brought up every memory of hiding from them. Every time I ran instead of fighting because I knew very well how dangerous they were, every feeling of fear, every instinct to survive… I poured it into my magic. It would only be temporary, but it would give me a head start.

The magic was dark in nature, so the energy that flooded the crystal was as deep a red as it had ever been. I wouldn't hurt the townspeople, but my brothers would take their frustrations out on them. It couldn't be helped because Livia was right; if they defeated Magnus, there would be no stopping them. Killing Magnus would give them a taste they wouldn't be able to resist.

When the city disappeared completely, I gaped. Panic rose until I felt my magic settle as the spell clicked into place. It was still there. The city was right in front of me, just invisible. All I could see was a field of grass and dirt.

The oddest part was that I had never had so much power before, and I had the sneaking suspicion that I was able to accomplish it because it was both light and dark magic. I wasn't hurting anyone, not even my brothers. At least, that was my justification for the part of me that couldn't stand harming people. After all, if I hadn't trapped my brothers, who knew what trouble they would cause looking for me?

I was still wondering why they were after me or how they got so close when I turned my staff back to the north. Once again, a deep orange light pulsed through the crystal. With one last glance behind me, I started walking north.

\*       \*       \*

I walked all day, and with no one to talk to, I was forced to think. The only thing I could think about was what Livia had told me and what Merlin had already known.

After an entire lifetime of wondering why I was such a failure, it was too much to learn that it wasn't completely my fault *and* that there was someone else like me at the same time. *Not just like me; she is family.* I stopped in the middle of the road. *I should have asked more questions or just… listened maybe.* I didn't want to, though. Even knowing that my mother would kill me without a second thought, it never occurred to me that she would lie to me. She knew all along that I was like this for a reason. Maybe she did think that I would have more dark magic because I was male, but she still could have told me *why* I was so different.

And then there was Merlin. The worst part wasn't that he only wanted to use me; it was that he didn't think I could handle knowing it. Then again, I didn't exactly handle it well. I knew he wanted his curse broken. *Then why didn't he let me try breaking his curse?*

Doubt, hope, anger, and confusion twisted around inside me until I just felt sick. What was I if not a sorcerer? Everyone was something… everyone except for my aunt and me. *Or are there more of us?* There were books about us, apparently, but that didn't mean there were others still alive. *Are there half mages, half seers? Maybe half magicians, half necromancers...* That was a terrifying thought; someone with control over the dead *and* illusionary magic was truly the last thing this world needed.

By the time the sun had set, I was exhausted, mostly mentally. I was also hungry, since I ate the last of my fish for breakfast, so I stopped at a small city. As I wandered through the town full of stone buildings and surrounded by wooden houses, I decided that the towns in Akadema were tiny.

I hesitated when a sign beside a sturdy wooden door promised food and a clean bed for a reasonable price. I didn't have any money, but I still had the jewelry I had picked up from the bandits on Akadema, so I went in. There were sturdy wooden tables around the room, a staircase in front of me leading up, and a long wooden bar to my left.

It was a much more respectable place than the taverns of Akadema. There weren't half-naked women serving drinks, drunk men trying their hardest to get into a brawl, or raucous laughter. On the contrary, there were only six customers, who were using their chairs as seats instead of clubs, enjoying polite conversation, and eating hearty meals.

The smell of roasted meat and fresh bread caused my stomach to growl. I approached the man behind the bar who was about the size of Bloodbath and possibly even more hairy.

"Good evening," I said, making my voice deeper than it naturally was. "I need a room and something to eat. What can I get for this?" I pulled one of the gold necklaces out of my bag. It was a locket that would be worth more to someone who liked pretty things, but I just wanted to eat and sleep in a comfortable bed.

The man's eyes widened. "Anything you want. Bread, stew, roast, vegetables, ale, wine… a woman."

No matter how confused I was, I wasn't interested in a woman I could buy, let alone one I could buy for a necklace. "Can you give me a room and send up food and drinking water? Any food you have ready will do, I'm not picky."

"Here is a key," he said, pulling one from under the counter and passing it to me. "Up the stairs, last door on your right."

"Thank you." I grabbed the key and started to turn, but he continued.

"I will ask you not to cause any problems here," he said, pointing to my staff. Although his voice was steady and deep, his tone was not impolite. "I have nothing against magic-users, but if you want to fight, you need to go outside or to the tavern. That's not the kind of business I run here."

"Do you get a lot of trouble from magic-users?"

"Not typically. Magic-users usually stick to their own kind around here. I'm just warning you that your gold doesn't mean I won't kick you out if you destroy something."

"Duly noted."

I went upstairs and found my room, which was simple, warm, and clean. Other than a small bed, there was a chest for clothes and a window. I sat on the bed, pulled out a book, and started reading. Soon, there was a knock on the door. When I answered it, a pretty woman gave me a mug of water and a plate of bread, cheese, and roast. I thanked her and shut the door. Although it smelled great, I was so hungry that I ate every bite without bothering to taste it.

When I was done, I set the dishes out in the hall, locked the door, undressed, and went to sleep.

*   *   *

I had more bad dreams about facing monsters, only this time I wasn't in a tower and Merlin wasn't coming to help me. The worst part was that Magnus's monster was a dragon and I had to fight it. I kept hearing my father's voice telling me that this was the last dragon and if I killed it, the extinction of the species would be my fault.

I forgot most of the details the moment I awoke. The dreams left me with dread and I felt like I was missing something very important. Trying to shake the feeling, I dressed, gathered everything up, and went downstairs. The same man was at the bar and along with the key, I handed him a gold bracelet that matched the necklace and asked for breakfast. Eggs and potatoes made a welcome treat after all the fish I had to eat on Bloodbath's ship.

"Are you a wizard or sorcerer?" he asked, wiping some dishes.

I sighed. "I'm a sorcerer." I couldn't very well say I was both; it wasn't normally a possibility. Fortunately, the man didn't say anything more. There were only a few other people in the room, so I easily overheard two men at a table near the window.

"Did you know that the king of Welsma sent his warriors to draft the men of Red Rock for a battle?"

"Yes. I heard he couldn't afford enough warriors, so he was looking to volunteer men against their will. Red Rock is about a day's south of here, right?"

"That's right. His men arrived at Red Rock yesterday afternoon, except the city was gone."

"What do you mean the city was gone?"

"I mean there was an open field where the city was supposed to be. I know it doesn't make sense, but it's true nonetheless."

I groaned and let my head fall to the bar next to my plate. I wasn't trying to curse the people, but I wasn't trying to save them. Apparently, even my neutral magic was white magic. *Maybe that's what's bothering me.* No, it was something bigger.

"Take some bread with you," the man behind the counter said, setting a loaf of bread wrapped in a thin cloth on the table.

"Thank you." I picked it up and started to put it in my bag… and froze. I had gotten books from Livia's library, so my bag should have been heavier than when I got to her castle. I quickly removed the books and set them on the table. Only then did I see what had been bothering me so much.

The syrus was missing. I knew I had it when I left Livia's castle, and that just made me sick to my stomach. The only time I could have lost it was when that boy in the city bumped into me and caused my bag to spill open. I replayed the event over and over but I couldn't remember seeing it to pick it up. There were other people around; it must have rolled out of sight.

"You just became pale as a ghost," the man said.

"I tried to get ahead of my brothers by trapping them temporarily, but I've just realized I forgot something I really need and now I have to go back to my brothers who are going to kill me painfully and slowly."

"Do you have another friend who can help you?"

"I did, but I kind of got mad at him for betraying me and left him."

"Well, that wasn't very smart."

"I know. When they get free, my brothers are going to come through here. They're not like me; they'll hurt people and destroy things just for fun. You might want to shut down for the next couple of days."

"Thank you for the warning."

I gathered the books back into the bag and went to the door, but when I opened it, I froze. Merlin was sitting right outside, looking very displeased. "What are you doing here?"

"*Did you honestly think I was going to let you get yourself killed?*"

"So you still don't think I can defeat Magnus on my own? After everything we've been through?"

"*I never said I did not believe you were capable; I just did not believe you would go through with it. Had I known you were the seventh son of the seventh son, that you had such a rare power, I would never have promised to teach you to be a sorcerer, because that was unfair to you.*"

"How was---" I was cut off as one of the two men who had been talking in the inn pushed me out of the doorway. "Sorry." My apology was unheard, because he ran away as soon as he spotted Merlin. I started walking south, since going after Magnus without the syrus was a waste of time. Merlin followed. "How was it unfair to promise to teach me to be a sorcerer?"

*"Because what you are is more important. Encouraging you to just be a sorcerer is repression."*

"But I just want to be a sorcerer. I want to be successful at it, but I would rather be a sorcerer than… not anything. What am I supposed to call myself now?"

*"Why must you call yourself something?"*

"Because people ask. Twice just yesterday I've been asked whether I'm a wizard or sorcerer. I don't know what to say now."

*"Then find something you want to be called and excel in that. You grew up believing that curses and manipulating people was your only future. Did you ever wish you could do something else?"*

I thought about it, and found myself grinning. "I like books. I like traveling, too. I could travel around and collect books. I could get a house and people could come and borrow books from me and then bring them back so others could read them too. I mean, it wouldn't be fair to have all the best books in the world and never let anyone else read them. What would that be called?"

*"A librarian, Ayden."*

"I like that. But no, that couldn't happen. No matter how much I may screw up as a sorcerer, I am still a Dracre, and my mother would never let me live as anything else."

*"Then you are determined to be a sorcerer?"*

"I'm determined to try. I'll defeat Magnus and my brothers if I have to. I will be a sorcerer, but not like my family, because I'll choose when to use sorcery and when not to. Maybe I'll use sorcery in a wizard way. Like, I would only help people when it benefits myself."

"*I foresee no terrible consequences deriving from that idea whatsoever,*" he said sarcastically.

"You're not a seer. Besides, I'm still mad at you for betraying me."

"*Then I will make it up to you. In the meantime, can we change your hair back now? It looks so odd.*"

"No. It pretty much saved my life when I ran into my brothers at Red Rock."

"Why are we going back the way we came from?"

"Long story. I forgot the syrus in the city a day south of here, and before leaving, I locked the city in an invisibility spell, which stopped my brothers from getting out. Now we have to go get it and probably face them. Then I found out that the city was about to be invaded and I ended up saving them from that."

"*Somehow I feel you just made the story much longer and more complicated than it would have been had you not shortened it.*"

We got back on the road and began the long journey back to face my brothers. "Thanks for coming after me and for facing my brothers with me."

"*Well, I admit it would have been easier had you not snuck out, but friends help each other, even if one of said friends forgets to act his age and locks himself in a room sometimes.*"

\*     \*     \*

We walked and walked. I told Merlin about what happened at Red Rock and then, with nothing else to do, we passed the time by telling fairytales. It occurred to me we should have been talking about Livia and what I learned, but I didn't want to get upset again.

When the sun was low in the sky, we finally reached the hill that overlooked the field where I knew the city was. "There it is. Well, it's there, but you can't see it. I'll have to break the spell, but first, a plan would be nice. The box will be in the middle of the road unless someone took it. Anyone in the city could have it. Furthermore, my brothers are there, and they're after me. I have no idea why or how they got so close."

*"It is most likely a blood call. Siblings are drawn together. As for a plan, I have one. I can sniff out the syrus the same way I found you. Watch for your brothers because I do not know their appearance."*

"They're hard to miss. I'll make us both invisible."

*"Tread carefully with such magic."*

"I know." I used both my wand and staff and visualized the two of us becoming invisible along with my bag, staff, and wand. My magic stirred slower than usual, as if it couldn't believe I was encouraging cooperation between the wand and staff. The magic was blue and trickled gently into both Merlin and me. I felt my skin tingle right before Merlin vanished. I reached out, unable to see myself at all, and felt his thick fur.

*"Because you cannot follow the sound of my voice, if we get separated and you need me, call out my name and stay still."*

I raised both my wand and staff again and focused on the spell I had put over the city, although it had not been my intention to make it invisible, it worked out in their favor. If my mother ever found out, I would be so dead a necromancer wouldn't even be able to resurrect me.

I felt the spell easily and since it was my own, breaking it was as simple as calling the magic back into me. As the city reappeared, there was a definite stain in the remnant energy; my brothers had tried to break out. They didn't try very hard, or they would have broken it easily, but they tried nonetheless. Maybe they were distracted by arguing with each other. I had always wondered what they would do if I weren't there for them to torment.

"Why are my brothers even looking for me?" I asked.

"*I suspect your mother must have sent them when she found out you left. Perhaps they don't know you're going after Magnus.*"

"No, she wouldn't risk the chance that someone would tip Magnus off. My brothers aren't very fast or wise; I'm sure they've told everyone they passed that they're going after him, and my mother knows that. She would tell them not to waste time until after they've defeated him."

"*Well, we should be off before someone leaves with the syrus.*"

I let my magic flood my wand again and white light wrapped around us. When it cleared, we were right back where I had been when I transported myself out. I was suddenly out of breath.

"*You are using a lot more magic than usual,*" Merlin warned. "*You have to build your endurance along with your magic.*"

I nodded, which I then realized was pointless because he couldn't see me. "Go look for the syrus. I'll keep an eye out for my brothers," I whispered.

"*Be safe.*" I didn't hear anything else, so I assumed he had left.

A moment later, dread welled up from deep inside me. It must have been my magic sensing my brothers' magic. A cruel laugh turned my blood cold, and then a spark in front of me caught fire. The fire spread to create a wide circle around me, only as high as my knees. It wasn't meant to burn me; there would be something worse trapping me inside.

Zeustrum, Bevras, Gibus, Febarin, Mikron, and Thaddeus all exited the tavern and surrounded me. Invisible or not, I was caught.

# CHAPTER 14

"I told you he'd come back," Thaddeus said.

He didn't look directly at me, though; none of them did. They couldn't see me. By then, everyone else in the city had shut themselves into their homes or businesses. Whether the Dracre reputation reached these lands or not, everyone recognized a sorcerer duel when they saw one.

Of course, this was more like a sorcerer execution.

"Why isn't he there?" Febarin asked accusingly.

Gibus rolled his eyes. "He obviously learned a spell that makes him invisible."

Zeustrum and Bevras shared a glare. "That is illusionary magic. Impossible. Ayden, explain yourself," Zeustrum demanded. His tone promised the beating of a lifetime if I didn't instantly obey.

"He must have picked up an enchanted item or something. It doesn't matter; he can't hold it for long."

I was so distracted by the fact that Zeustrum was right— invisibility was illusionary magic and therefor impossible for a sorcerer to do— that I didn't realize what Gibus said until I felt the lethargy start to drag on my magic. This was one of their favorite curses; the circle would draw on my magic until any spell I cast was broken, including my invisibility.

I sighed and allowed the magic over me, my bag, my wand, and my staff to fall. To my brothers, it would look like I gave up, but I really just wanted to put all my strength into keeping Merlin hidden for as long as possible.

Bevras's eyes widened. "Your hair! How did you get your hair to stay black?"

"Never mind that," Zeustrum dismissed. "You are in a lot of trouble, little brother."

"Why were you looking for me?"

Thaddeus scoffed. "Are you serious? You thought you could go and warn Magnus about us and we wouldn't stop you?"

I gaped. "You thought I was trying to warn Magnus you were going after him?!" My screech of outrage might have been a little hysterical. They did everything they could to humiliate me and torment me just because I wasn't like them, but it never crossed my mind that they would think I was a traitor.

Zeustrum's eyes narrowed. "Why else would you have run away the night before we were sent to defeat him?"

"I was going after him myself! I wanted to defeat him alone to prove to Mother that I'm just as powerful a sorcerer as you all!"

"Alone? Are you insane?" Mikron sneered. "Not even one of us could defeat him alone." Zeustrum and Bevras glared at him. "Okay, maybe Zeus and Bev could, but certainly not you. You could have just begged Mother to let you go with us."

"Oh, yes, like I went with you on that hunting trip last summer?" They all laughed at the memory and my face flushed. They made it a game to see which of them could kill me first until I managed to escape and return home. Mother ridiculed me for days and then tried to send me back to them. To my surprise, Mikron and Thaddeus were faking their laughter. I turned to my oldest brother because he was the only one the others would listen to. "Zeus, please, just let me go."

"Why would I want to do that?"

An idea was forming in my head as the words came out of my mouth. "Because I have something you want more than me dead." As if it knew my plan, the crystal on my staff pulsed with a deep, dark red glow. All my brothers' eyes fixed on it. "This is not only the most powerful sorcerer staff that has ever existed; it can also show you the way to Magnus."

"How?"

I lowered it to point at them, but none of them flinched because their faith in the circle around me was absolute, unlike their faith in me, apparently. However, I had enough magic left since I dropped my invisibility. When I pointed the crystal to the north, it pulsed. Zeustrum's eyes lit up with interest.

"And why shouldn't we just take it from you and kill you?"

"You can't get it without dropping your circle. If you let me go, you can always come up with a way to use me later as bait, a decoy, or whatever. Drop your circle and take the staff. Just look away for a moment so I can run."

Thaddeus went up to him and whispered something in his ear. His expression showed utter shock for just an instant before he schooled it. "Alright. Give me the staff and run. Run as fast and as far away as you can and never return. If I ever see your nuisance face again, it will be the last time."

Curiosity burned inside me; Zeus never changed his mind. Whatever Thaddeus had said, it was huge.

The circle fell and Zeustrum stepped forward. I held my wand in my left hand and handed my staff to him with my right. Zeustrum would never take my wand for himself, but he also wouldn't consider it a threat worth disarming me of. As soon as he took the staff, Bevras and Febarin each grabbed my arms to restrain me.

I didn't fight them. "Dishonest to the end. You may end up on top, but you'll be alone."

He smirked. "That never once mattered to me."

"You really don't want to do this."

"I really do." He aimed the staff at me and pure black magic burst from the crystal.

At the same time, white magic was drawn out of me, through the wand, and into the staff. The black magic and white magic were one for just an instant, each swirling around each other in a stream between the wand and staff. It was Zeus's magic, but it was my staff, and a magic staff would never hurt its true master.

The magic struck Bevras and Febarin like black lightning and through the staff, it simultaneously spread down the length of the staff to reach Zeustrum. He convulsed, like the two beside me did, but they collapsed onto the ground and he only went to his knees. The magic then spread to Gibus and Mikron. Thaddeus was nowhere to be seen.

Once all my brothers except for Thaddeus were unmoving and unconscious, the magic stopped. I picked up my staff, oddly upset by the fact that the crystal was pure black. Apparently, my wand was disgruntled as well, because it sent a painful spark up my arm, through my heart, down the other arm, and into the staff. I shuddered, but the crystal lightened considerably, so it was worth the physical discomfort.

*"That was quite the display of bravery,"* Merlin said.

He was still invisible, so I didn't bother looking for him. "Not hardly. I would have let him go if he hadn't tried to kill me. That's weakness."

*"Mercy is not weakness. You knew the staff would reverse the attack and you tried to talk him out of using it. Showing yourself to them was bravery, and maintaining the spell over me when you needed the power most was friendship. You proved you are a better man than any of your brothers, sorcerer or otherwise."*

"Did you get the syrus?"

*"I did."*

The battle was over and people began peeking out their doors and windows to see how much damage there was. Since it would look to them like I was talking to myself, I dropped the spell. Merlin appeared right in front of me with the syrus at his feet. "Was the invisibility spell even helpful to you at all?"

*"It was very helpful. A merchant had found it and tried to sell it. I had to sneak into his shop and take it back. When I returned, I considered stepping in, but by then, your brother had already taken the staff and I knew how the situation would play out. I think you did very well."*

At that moment, people started returning to the streets, seeing my brothers on the ground, and cheering. They were cheering because they thought my brothers were dead. I couldn't stop the anger from welling up inside. "What is wrong with you people?" I asked. "What could you possibly have to be happy about seeing them on the ground like this?"

Confused muttering replaced the cheering. "They were threatening the city," one woman said.

"How? Other than being obnoxious hooligans, what did they actually do?" I saw no damage to the city, no piles of bodies, and no rivers of blood.

The crowd looked even more confused. "Well, they were sorcerers."

I felt... much less shocked than I should have. Yes, that kind of thinking was rare where I was from, but Merlin seemed to be of the mind that people didn't like sorcerers. There were some places where people were suspicious of magic-users, and some where they only liked particular magic-users, but on most lands, everyone was considered equal.

The people of Akadema never shunned wizards, but there were no wizards living there, so the people turned to sorcerers like my family or another magic-user. Sorcerers were shadier, but people went to them for help more than wizards because, if nothing else, sorcerers were more trustworthy. Sorcerers would always be willing to get their hands dirty for the right price, and they valued repeat business. Wizards never accepted coin, so they only helped someone if they felt it was their duty.

"*I* am a sorcerer! Sentence people for their actions, not for being alive! If they've done something to you or your family, you can cheer when they fall. Otherwise, act like people instead of bloodthirsty animals and show sympathy for a fallen man." The villagers looked properly chastised and I was about to continue when Zeustrum started to move. "That being said, they're dangerous and angry so run and hide!" I picked up the syrus, stuffed it into my bag, and then transported us back to the hilltop.

"*We must hurry; they will be able to follow us. How far can you transport us?*"

"I'm okay to transport us to somewhere I can see. If I can't see where we're going, we could end up anywhere."

"*Can you see the previous city in your memory and take us back there?*"

"I'm not sure. It would be dangerous to try."

"*More dangerous than your brothers if they catch up to us?*"

"No." *At least, I really hope not.* I closed my eyes and focused on the inn I had stayed at. I focused on the bar, the tables, and the comforting scent. The only reason I didn't think of the owner was because I didn't know if he would be there or not and I didn't want it to mess me up. Unfortunately, I still hadn't recovered from all the magic I used and the circle that drained what was left.

I sensed that something went wrong, so I wasn't surprised to open my eyes and find myself alone in the dark. "Merlin?" I whispered. No answer. I knew my magic had transported him because I felt it, but there was no telling where he was. Or where I was, for that matter.

Even though I was almost painfully exhausted of magic, I still managed to push enough into my wand to light the tip and bathe the room in a dim glow. It was a small study filled with books of all things! I knew then why my spell went wrong; I needed more than magic to defeat my enemy. I started searching the shelves for anything that could help me.

"*Ayden, are you okay?*" Merlin asked.

Once again, I answered without thinking about it. "*I seem to be. What about you?*" It was a very strange phenomenon. I thought the words so strongly that I could hear my own voice out loud, yet I hadn't opened my mouth.

"*I am safe for the moment, only... I appear to be in a young lady's bedroom and she is very upset to see me, quite possibly because she has no clothes on. Furthermore, it is difficult to open the door with paws.*"

I saw a book on magical monsters. Since Livia said there would be a monster at Magnus's castle, I grabbed it, shoved it into my bag, and left the last of my gold jewelry on the shelf in its place. Then I focused my magic into both my wand and staff to transport me to Merlin. The first thing I saw when the white magic faded was a very naked woman. She stopped screaming when she saw me.

"Hello. I'm Ayden."

"*Open the door!*" Merlin demanded.

"Sorry, I'm just here to get my wolf." When I opened the door, Merlin rushed out. I followed reluctantly, but not so slowly that the woman had time to respond.

We were now out on the main road of the city. I knew it was the right city because I recognized the inn I had stayed at the previous night. And then I suddenly felt so sick that I had to rush over to the side of the road and throw up.

"*You are going to cripple yourself if you continue doing magic without food and rest. I suggest we stop for the night.*"

"But my brothers…"

*"They most likely have no idea where this town is and will therefore have to walk. I also suspect that they will not travel at night."*

"Alright." I really didn't want to argue. All I wanted to do was go to sleep. "Where should we sleep?" Lightning crackled in the sky right before it opened up and dumped heavy rain. "That's just what we need."

*"You need to be in a bed and out of the weather. We do not know how many more days our travels will take and you must be well-rested for what we will soon face."*

"We have no money."

*"After a night of rest and some food, you should be in good shape. You of all people should know that everyone could use some magical assistance. With sorcery and wizardry, surely you can find someone with a spare bed who would accept something other than money in return."*

I thought about it and nodded. "We might as well try the innkeeper." We entered the inn to find the same man as before behind the bar. I wondered if he was there all day, every day.

"Welcome back," he said kindly. He pulled a small towel from somewhere behind the bar and handed it to me.

"Thank you." I used the towel to dry my hair. It wasn't terribly cold outside and it was warm inside, so I wasn't worried about getting sick. When I started trying to pat-dry my clothes, I noticed he was staring at my hair. "What?"

"Your hair is changing color."

"What? Oh, no, the ink!"

*"Worry about your hair later,"* Merlin said.

"Right. I'm out of gold and I don't have anything to trade for, but I really want to sleep inside. Is there any magic you need?"

He pursed his lips and leaned on the bar. "Can't say that there is. Tell you what, though," he said, pointing to another man sitting alone at a table by the window. "I bet he could use some help, and he might have the money to pay."

"Thanks," I said. I cautiously approached the man. He was facing away from me, so I couldn't see his face and get an idea what kind of man he was. He must have heard me when I was about halfway across the room because he turned. "Bralyn?!"

He stood. "Yes, it's me. You ran away." He wasn't happy.

I scowled. "I was angry."

His expression softened a little. "I know, but I wasn't the one who lied to you, so you should have at least taken me with you. It took me two days to get here."

I looked at Merlin. "*I run faster as a wolf than he does as a man. If he had shifted, it would have taken him just as long because he would have been sneezing the entire way. Ask him how he found you.*"

I did, and Bralyn answered, "Livia. She showed me where you were heading through her mirror. I also saw your confrontation with your brothers. You need to do something about your hair. Come on, I already got us a room."

We went up to his room, which was the same one I had the night before. Once we were alone, I stripped off my clothes and changed into the only spare shirt and pants

I had, then laid my wet robe and clothes out on the chest to dry.

Next, I used the ink-stained towel to dry my staff and wand. "How bad is my hair?" I asked.

Bralyn grimaced. "It's pretty bad. You would be better off washing it out. It's all splotchy and gray."

I wouldn't say I was vain, but Mother always said we only had one chance to make a first impression. It was better to face Magnus with my normal color than to face him with splotchy gray, black, and blond hair. Bralyn left to get a bucket and cloth to wash out the rest of the ink. "I guess it was a waste of time to use the ink in the first place," I said.

*"Not necessarily. Your brothers probably would have recognized you by your hair and robe in Red Rock the first time, when you would not have had the time to escape. Also, it has reaffirmed in my mind that you look better blond. The black is too severe."*

I sighed. I knew that; I had seen my hair in mirrors after my mother made it black. The fact that it always reverted to blond when I did magic was probably a good thing.

Bralyn returned, filled the bucket with rainwater from the window, and helped me wash the rest of the ink out. Once that was done, he pulled a cloth sack off his belt. "Livia said to give this to you."

"Did she apologize for locking us up?" I asked, dropping my towel and taking the pouch from him.

"No, she insisted she was trying to help us. She said this was called a dragon's eye and that it belonged to your father's father."

"That's where I recognized it from!" I said, pulling the multi-colored crystal out of the pouch. "I saw it in one of my father's books when he was teaching me to read. It has to do with dragon training. I have no idea what it does, only that it's powerful." It felt almost warm in my hands.

"*I can sense the magic in that*," Merlin said.

"Can you sense what kind it is? Like sorcery or wizardry?"

"*I can, and it is nothing as simple as that. This is dragon magic.*"

*   *   *

We were back on the road heading north by sunrise and I felt much better. Fortunately, although the ground was muddy, the rain hadn't lasted the night. With a vast amount of walking to do, I went over the different monsters that the book I found talked about. Basically, we tried to memorize a plan of attack for each of the creatures we faced. I stopped when I reached the page on dragons. "I was serious about what I said before; I'm not going to fight a dragon," I told Merlin. "Dragons are amazing creatures that have been unjustly hunted to near extinction, if not full extinction."

"*What if Magnus's creature is a dragon?*"

"Then we'll come up with something else. I am against fighting dragons." I turned the page stubbornly. "How about I skip the ones that a wizard wouldn't use? There's a reptile that is about the size of a bear and spits acid. No wizard would keep such a vulgar guardian, so we shouldn't waste time learning about it."

"*There is no such thing as wasting time learning something*," Merlin lectured.

"Fine. It spits acid, so if we face it, we'll die." I turned the page and laughed. "This one emits radiation, so we would die." I turned the page again. "Stuns its victims with a pulsating light and eats them, so we'd die."

"Are there any nice magical monsters in there?" Bralyn asked.

"The unicorn," I said.

"Well, I wouldn't want to get impaled by its horn."

"But they're friendly."

"Only if you're a child or virgin," he said. I blushed and turned the page. "Don't worry; I'm a trained warrior. I have faced many monsters and they were all the same in one way."

"What's that?"

"They all lost to me."

That was simultaneously the most ghastly and inspiring thing I heard since I left home.

*   *   *

We walked until the sun was high in the sky and the road was long gone. That was when we came to a cliff. "Well, this is a problem." The cliff was basically a huge hole in the ground. My staff pulsed violently. "I don't understand. The staff is acting like the castle is right here."

*"Ayden, I sense very powerful magic. I am going to teach you something that is not sorcery or wizardry. Close your eyes."* I closed them without arguing. *"Do you know how when you exhale on a cold day, you can see your breath?"*

"Yes."

"Yes what?" Bralyn asked.

"I'm talking to Merlin."

*"Imagine that, but imagine it is your magic being exhaled."*

"That's a waste of magic," I protested.

*"No, it is not, because you are going to pull it back into yourself soon. Do as I say. Inhale deeply, as deeply as you possibly can, until you feel like you will choke on it, and then hold it... Good. Now let it out, and as you do, release your magic along with your breath. Exhale every bit of air in your lungs and wait for as long as you can to inhale. Hold... hold... and breathe. Imagine that as you inhale, you are inhaling the magic."*

I did as he said and when my lungs were almost refilled, an image came to mind. It was as unclear as a cloud, but there was definitely something massive right in front of me. "What is that?"

*"It will become clearer with practice. What you see before you is something shielded in magic."*

"The castle?"

*"Most definitely."*

"What's going on?" Bralyn asked.

In answer, I pocketed my wand, aimed the staff in front of me, and released my magic. A gust of wind and red magic swirled together and crashed into the open air in front of me. I heard the sound of metal creaking before the invisible gates opened... revealing a massive wizard's castle.

# CHAPTER 15

"It's a castle in an invisible bubble," Bralyn said needlessly.

"Yes, it is."

"The castle of Magnus the Great is in an invisible bubble."

"Yes."

"The castle of Magnus the Great that is guarded by a monster."

"Right, maybe we should be careful. I knew he was powerful, but I didn't know a person could be *this* powerful. Our plan isn't going to work. We're all going to die."

"*Stop being so negative*," Merlin said.

"Fine." I gave him my best fake smile. "We're all going to die," I said with a sarcastically joyous tone.

"*That is better.*"

"Never enter a battle expecting to lose," Bralyn admonished. "That is the surest way to fail."

Not wanting to get a lecture from Bralyn, I asked the next question in Merlin's mind. *"What if the monster is invisible like the castle?"*

*"That is unlikely."*

*"Why?"*

*"Because I believe that is the monster coming towards us now."*

I looked back through the gates and groaned. It was definitely not a dragon.

Of all the magical creatures I had ever heard of, this was the second-worst one. Aside from being terrifying in appearance, strong, and fast, it was also invulnerable to magic. It had the head and body of a lion with large tan-colored, feather wings and a goat's head protruding from its back, and a snake for a tail. The description of the creature sounded ridiculous, as if the gods were bored one day and decided to create a combination that couldn't possibly make sense. I imagined even they were shocked at how perfectly designed the chimera was against a magical opponent.

It had spectacular eyesight when there was light and could see body heat in pitch blackness. The creature's sense of smell was so precise that people believed it could smell what someone was going to do before they did it. It also had the strength of a lion and the speed of a serpent. It's only natural enemy was the dragon.

The creature landed right outside the invisible gates, which was way too close to us as far as I was concerned. One thing the legends couldn't decide on was whether or not the beast breathed fire. If it could, we were as good as cooked already.

Bralyn groaned as he drew the sword at his side. "Why did it have to have fur?" He spoke quietly, obviously not meaning for me to have heard him. Then his expression hardened with determination, but I thought some of it might have been for show. "I will face this---"

"Absolutely not," I interrupted. "That thing has a serpent as its tail."

"Don't tell me you want to *reason* with it," he said.

"I'm not a complete idiot." I raised my wand and staff up above me like I had when I was creating the monkey monster and I summoned it back. Although I was here for sinister reasons, I wasn't concerned whether I was using sorcery or wizardry this time. I was summoning my monster both to defeat the chimera and to protect myself and my friends. At the same time, my magic was no shallower than it was when I created the monkey.

Once again, white magic from my wand and red magic from the staff clashed in the middle. Out of the swirling magic formed a black shape that grew and solidified into my flying monkey, still with tentacles. *If I'm very lucky, maybe the strangeness of my creature will scare off the chimera.*

The chimera took one look at the monkey and roared.

*I'm not that lucky.*

The monkey didn't need any instructions; he swooped down on the chimera like they were mortal enemies. His tentacles wrapped around the chimera's thick lion neck, but before his claws could scratch at the chimera's eyes, he had to dodge the serpent. The chimera had no known weaknesses.

Except dragons.

"*I do not think the monkey is going to cut it this time,*" Merlin said.

"I don't think there's anything that can." My monster wasn't going to give up too easily, though. He slashed at the serpent with his sharp claws while he distracted the goat and lion heads with his tentacles. He wasn't winning, but he wasn't going down, either. "Bralyn, wait," I said when the warrior started to advance on the battle. "My monster needs room to fight the chimera without someone getting in the way." Without giving him a chance to argue, I set my wand and staff aside and pulled the syrus out of my bag. It popped open easily. There was no glowing light, though, just a red velvet lining. "How do I make this work?"

"*The latch on the front, do you see it?*"

"Yes."

"*Prick your finger, wipe your blood on the latch while the lock is open, and do the reverse of what you did to open it.*"

"The reverse of what I did to open it? I don't know what I did."

"Shouldn't you have discussed this before?" Bralyn asked, not taking his eyes off the fight.

"Yes, probably, but I didn't know it would need to be activated." I pulled the small knife from my bag and cut my finger. It stung as I wiped my blood on the small silver latch. It was a simple lock. There was a slim, round piece of metal on the base of the chest that rotated. I would close the latch over it so that the round piece would stick through, then twist it so that the latch wouldn't open.

"*Read the inscription on the front,*" Merlin instructed.

"But I already read it."

"*Stop arguing. We are running out of time.*"

Without closing it, I checked every spot on the chest, but there wasn't an inscription. "It's gone!" I didn't wait for him to explain it to me, though. I picked up my wand and waved it at the syrus. *Reveal your secrets.*

To my surprise, that worked; words appeared on the front of it.

*The greatest victory is that which requires no battle.*

I frowned, because that was considerably less substantial than the previous inscription. "What's with the random wisdom? Was this made by mages or something?"

*"The magic of the syrus is older and greater than mine, and I know not where it came from."*

"Can't you just say you don't know? Is it ready now?"

*"No, there is one more requirement; you must include a genetic sample of the creature or person you wish to imprison. You need blood, fur, a claw, or anything that is a part of the creature's body. Place it inside the syrus and it will fully charge."*

"Charge? What does that mean?"

*"Think of it like lightning forming before it strikes. After that, you need only to get the creature close enough."*

"How close?"

*"I cannot be sure."*

"Great. How do I get the blood?"

"What blood?" Bralyn asked.

"I need the chimera's blood to make the syrus work."

"Leave that to me." He charged into the battle.

"But what about your allergies?" I yelled after him. I considered making him invisible, but the chimera would be able to see his body heat anyway. By then, it was too late. The monkey was distracting all three heads, giving Bralyn the opportunity to strike. He was fast; fast enough to do the warrior reputation proud. As easily as if it were holding still, Bralyn cut off the serpent head.

The chimera's scream was horrific and I felt deep pity. It was only doing its job and the snake was a vital part of its self-defense. Now, if we didn't defeat it, another enemy would. Then the lion head bit down on one of my monkey's tentacles and tore it off, which made me angry. I raised my staff, about to defend the monkey, when Bralyn sneezed all over the chimera.

Wiping his nose with one hand, he harnessed his sword and reached for the snake head. The chimera swiped at Bralyn's head, but the monkey rammed into his larger opponent's side, sending them both rolling away from the warrior. Bralyn got the head, returned to us, and handed it to me. "Will this do?"

Merlin dipped his head in a nod.

I set my staff down and pocketed my wand. "We just toss it in?" I asked, taking it from Bralyn with a shudder. The scales were dark green, dry, and smooth, while the neck itself was wider than my own body. The head was about the size of Bralyn's in his bear form. I had no doubt the monster could swallow me whole if it were still alive.

*"You only need some of the blood,"* the wolf corrected.

I held it with both hands over the syrus. It was draining blood in a very gory fashion, so Merlin told me after just a moment that it was enough.

"This would make a fine trophy for your sorcery collection," Bralyn said as he took it from me. "Perhaps its venom would be useful as a potion ingredient."

"I'm not touching that again." The inside of the chest began to glow, the light afternoon breeze suddenly turned violent, and the sky darkened with angry clouds. "Is this normal?" I asked, having to yell to be heard over the wind. Even though Akadema rarely had summer storms, I highly suspected this was magic-related.

*"I have only been through this once and I was not focused on the details at the time. I suggest getting out from between the syrus and the chimera."*

When my monkey creature howled in pain, we turned back to the battle and discovered how bad the situation really was. The snake head had not only grown back, it grew two heads! The chimera now had two snake tails and my poor monkey didn't stand a chance. Claws, teeth, and horns were making short work of my monster, so I acted on instinct.

I grabbed my staff, pulled my wand out of my pocket, and held them out. This time, I didn't care if I lost control of my creature; I just wouldn't let him suffer anymore. I let my magic shape itself around my desire, which was to protect the creature I had created. Whether it was sorcery or wizardry or whatever, I didn't care.

The red magic from my staff was more orange than usual and the white magic from my wand was bluer, but when the two energies met, they formed a deep gray storm cloud. I felt a tingling sensation in my chest as if magic was crawling across my skin. My own magic was pouring from me, into the magical instruments, out into the cloud, back into the wand and staff, and back into me. I thought it was a mistake at first, or that I wasn't powerful enough to pull off what I needed to do. However, as the magic grew hotter, flowed faster, and felt heavier all at once, I realized what was happening. I didn't understand it, but I knew what it was.

My magic was gaining a sort of buildup and becoming more potent by folding over on itself. I was also starting to shake. As strong as my body might have felt at that moment, I couldn't move, and I knew the energy inside me was the only thing holding me together. I might as well have been an empty shell with only magic to prevent me from breaking. It was a miserable feeling, but also somehow familiar. It was like being a part of something so much more important by only existing as an extension of that.

I loved magic. It was all I had, all I knew, and the only thing no one could take away from me.

But it wasn't worth this. It wasn't worth being empty.

Merlin had said that no sorcerer was happy. Was any wizard happy? Was anyone who had to live in a standardized way happy? I didn't want to be told I couldn't help my friends because it wasn't sorcery, or that I couldn't create a monkey monster because it wasn't wizardry. I wanted to read my books and go on adventures and learn great and terrible magic.

I wanted the choice.

At that moment, I chose to cast aside the rules and constraints of wizards and sorcerers and defeat the foolish chimera who dared to injure my monkey monster.

I wasn't even aware of what was forming in the cloud until it grew to such great proportions that it towered over me, and then, when I realized it, I knew it couldn't have been anything else. Somehow, with some power I couldn't have created myself, I had conjured a dragon.

The majestic creature was not as large as some I had read about, but it was huge nonetheless. Its wings were ominously angular. They were as red as fresh blood on the outward side and stone-gray on the inward side. Its body looked like gray rocks had been half melted together to form its armor. Its head was narrow and angular with two horns curving backward on the top of its head. Its eyes glowed with the same sinister reddish-orange as the magic from my crystal.

While I stood there in stunned silence like a fool, the dragon was assessing the situation. He didn't wait for my command before turning and attacking the chimera. When he flapped his wings, they emitted smoke as if they were on fire. The dragon swooped down on the chimera without a shred of fear. It was the chimera's turn to be afraid.

Although the serpent bit at the dragon's wings and stone flesh, it wasn't able to break through the armor. The dragon's talons, however, tore easily through the lion's hide. "Don't kill it!" I warned. "Just get it close to the syrus."

The dragon gave me an irritated scowl and snorted out a puff of smoke, but did as I demanded. He hooked his claws into the chimera's wings and began dragging the thrashing monster towards the syrus. Unfortunately, the energy inside me was still building. I felt like the dragon was feeding off my own magic, and if I let go for even an instant, the dragon would turn on me.

That was strange, because I shouldn't have had that much magic in me.

The chimera broke away from the dragon, bringing my attention back to the battle. Both the dragon and chimera took off into the air, but that only gave the dragon an even bigger advantage. Bigger, as in he was four times larger than the chimera. They dived, clawed, and bit at each other for a while before the chimera turned and tried to fly away. That was when the dragon decided to stop playing.

The energy inside me finally broke and I felt like all my bones, organs, blood, and skin were just going to burn away into ash. I could feel the heartbeats of the dragon inside of me. My father told me they had two hearts, but I had always thought that was just a myth.

The dragon opened its mouth wide and I expected fire to emerge. It wasn't fire, though. Blindingly bright lightning struck the chimera and the poor creature crashed to the ground hard. It didn't move again. Unfortunately, I couldn't move either. When the dragon used the lightning, I felt like it was pulled through me into him. Every part of my body hurt so much I couldn't even breathe.

The dragon dragged the unresisting monster towards the syrus and when it was close, the light of the chest reached out for the smaller beast. The chimera seemed to dissolve into dust and was absorbed into the syrus. Once the enemy was fully inside, the lid snapped shut and the lock turned.

No longer needed, the dragon also vanished into dark smoke, which then swirled around me faster and faster before flowing into the crystal of my staff. Only then did my own energy return to me in great waves. It felt cool and soothing against the heat left inside me, like a dozen healing potions at once. The internal damage caused by conjuring and controlling a dragon was undone. I could breathe again.

I also collapsed because I was shaking so hard, but I was alive. In fact, I felt kind of great. Bralyn stared at the spot where the dragon had disappeared, a mixture of confusion and awe on his face. Merlin nudged me in the arm, obviously concerned.

"I'm okay, I think. I just don't have a clue what happened."

"*Check the dragon's eye.*"

Somehow, I had managed to hold onto my staff and wand the entire time, and now I had to pry my fingers open to let go. Carefully, as my fingers were numb, I pulled the dragon's eye out of my pocket and gaped. The crystal was completely clear. I tried the breathing trick Merlin had taught me to see the invisible castle, but it didn't work; I couldn't see the magic in the crystal.

"*It is empty,*" Merlin said.

"What do you mean, empty?"

"*All of the magic that was inside it last night is gone.*"

I was about to ask where it went, when I looked at my staff. The crystal on my staff was now a deep, dark blue, but it reflected shards of rainbow colors in the sunlight like an opal. "Please don't tell me that's what I think it is."

"*I believe so. It appears that your sorcerer's staff is now a dragon staff.*"

"Does that mean I can't do sorcery anymore?" Not that I could do it before.

"*No. I expect that it will produce the same magic, except for when you summon a dragon. I suggest you find out exactly what it does before you do any more conjuring.*"

"Speaking of…" I looked around for my monkey monster, but it was gone. "Where's my monkey?"

"*He vanished when your dragon took over in the fight. He is probably healing.*"

"We did it!" Bralyn said, unaware and unconcerned with mine and Merlin's conversation.

"Yes, we trapped him. Now how are we supposed to trap Magnus?" I asked, getting back to my feet. I had to use the staff to brace myself. They both thought for a moment. "If we open the syrus to trap Magnus in it, will the monster escape?"

"*Yes. Only one soul can be trapped at a time,*" Merlin answered.

Before any of us could come up with another idea, the invisibility spell around the castle disappeared, the ground rumbled ominously, and white magic wrapped around us, blocking out everything.

*That's it? We worked so hard to get here and defeated the monster and now we're caught? I even faced my brothers!* When the light faded, we were in the throne room of a castle. It was a wizard's castle with absolutely no hint of dark magic.

And it was identical to Livia's castle, right down to the gold artwork.

Standing right in front of me was Magnus, the greatest wizard of Caldaca. He was tall— taller than any person I had ever met, but not like a troll. Although his white robes were thick, I could tell he was quite thin, even to the point where I would call him frail. In fact, he was old enough in appearance that he should have been taken care of by his children. His hair and beard were as long and white as his robe, his eyes were the lightest blue, and his wrinkles had wrinkles of their own. Then again, he was a wizard, so there was no telling how old he really was.

Perhaps due to his fragile appearance or possibly out of desperation, I thrust out my staff, an instant away from calling my exhausted monkey to fight once more. Magnus was faster. A wizard staff, eerily similar to mine, appeared in his hand. This staff was the same height and there was a crystal at the top, but the wood was a little lighter, the sigils were silver instead of gold, and the crystal was clear.

The wizard aimed his staff threateningly at mine and pure white magic emerged. To my shock, it shielded him instead of attacking me. I shouldn't have been surprised, though; wizards never attacked first. "Wait, Ayden!" he said.

That surprised me in a completely different way. "How do you know my name?"

"I have been waiting for you since you left your mother's home. I watched your journey."

I groaned. "You have a magic mirror like Livia, don't you?"

He frowned at me like I had insulted him. "Of course not, Ayden. Only sorcerers have magic mirrors. I use magic to see through my minion's eyes."

"Minion?"

"Yes, my minion, Fluffy."

His minion appeared on his shoulder and I squeaked a little. It was a fluffy black kitten with small bat wings. I didn't know whether to be awed by the cuteness or disturbed by the fact that this wizard was watching me for days. "Why were you watching me? How did you know I was coming?"

"A seer told me a long time ago that you would come. I have waited patiently for you to rescue me."

I felt something deep and cold settle in my stomach. "To what?"

"To rescue me from the chimera that trapped me here in my castle."

"The chimera that what?"

"You came to rescue me, didn't you? I was told by the seer that a young man born of sorcerers with both dark and light magic would come to help me when no one else was brave enough."

Merlin and Bralyn looked at me, watching for my reaction. I waited for the anger and horror to build up inside me, for my staff to curse the wizard, for anything... and then I sighed. "Fine. Whatever. I give up. I am the most pathetic sorcerer that has ever existed and whatever. I'll be a librarian."

"Okay..." He frowned worriedly, as if he was no longer sure of my mental health. I wasn't too sure either anymore.

"If you're the most powerful wizard of Caldaca, why were you unable to fight the chimera?"

"Not even a wizard as powerful as me could do much against a creature that was invulnerable to magic. And I'm glad you changed your hair back to blond; the black didn't suit you."

"You're taking this well," Bralyn said to me. "Isn't your mother going to kill you?"

"Yes, if my brothers don't first. They're still coming here."

"Why would your brothers come here?" Magnus asked.

I gave him my best look of disbelief. "My mother sent them to kill you. How could you not know that? Did you just spy on me and completely disregard the six more powerful sorcerers who were also heading your way?"

"Yes, of course. They weren't important. They could never have gotten rid of the chimera."

"Why not?"

"Because as powerful as they are, they're just sorcerers. All they know how to use is their magic, and a chimera cannot be defeated by magic."

"Then you won't have any trouble when they come to fight you?" Bralyn asked.

"No matter how strong I am, they're still six highly trained sorcerers against one wizard."

Bralyn and Merlin looked at me again and I just sighed because it really shouldn't have been surprising at all. It was like my brothers knew this was coming all along. And maybe, somewhere deep inside, I did as well. I didn't want to hurt people, but I didn't want to be a wizard, either. For the first time, I considered that it was better for me to be good at being me than a failure at being what everyone else wanted me to be.

That meant I was going to have to face my brothers for good, and there was only one way I would come out of that alive; I had to make it a fair fight. Wizard or not, Magnus would make a very strong ally, and we had a common enemy. "I guess we need a plan then."

"*A sorcerer would let Magnus face them alone to try to kill off as many of his enemies as possible,*" Merlin advised.

I nodded. "Sorcerers aren't known for teamwork."

"We're going to help?" Bralyn asked, looking a little excited.

"That's the only honorable way to do this, and the best chance for all of us to make it out alive. I know my brothers better than anyone."

# CHAPTER 16

It did not take long to come up with a plan. The first thing we needed was an advanced warning. Fortunately, we had Fluffy. Through his minion's eyes, Magnus saw them making their way down the same road I had followed and estimated their arrival at about sunset. Then we had to put in traps for our defense.

The main conflict we had to work through was the fact that I refused to kill my brothers no matter how bad they were. Merlin had the solution to this. While Magnus placed the proper stones and candles in the courtyard in front of the castle, Merlin directed me on the final part of the plan. I had bowls of ink, red and blue paint, and water. I painted sigils and circles on the wooden floor of the castle's main room, which Magnus had no objection to whatsoever.

As I worked, I also asked Merlin to explain why the crystal on my staff kept changing colors. Apparently, the staff had been stained with the vileness of the people who had used it over the years. The more white magic I used, the more pure it became. However, my magic wasn't entirely pure. When I stopped fighting the "neutral" magic inside me, the wand and staff bonded completely. Now they could both do whatever magic I needed, but the wand was more portable and the staff was more powerful. However, Merlin didn't know what the dragon's eye that had fused into the crystal would do.

I asked Magnus if he knew anything about it. He said he'd heard of the dragon's eye crystals before, but what they actually did was a closely-guarded secret of the dragon trainers. Unfortunately, other than my father, I didn't know any dragon trainers, and if it was so secret, the answer wouldn't be in just any old book.

Magnus said he already had suitable enchantments embedded into the ground outside, which was why he transported us to him instead of letting us walk through it. The stones and candles were apparently to set the boundaries of the trap, because otherwise the magic would be too wild. I was shocked that a wizard would have a trap in place just in case he was attacked. That seemed so non-wizard-like to me, but when I expressed this to Merlin, he gave me a blank stare.

It was sunset when my brothers arrived. I watched at the window as they entered through the gates. Although I was careful to stay out of sight, they were arrogant enough that they didn't bother looking up. I picked up my staff, focused on the presence of my monster, and pulled on that sensation until he felt me calling him. My staff created blue magic that flowed upward into the air. Out of that, the monkey monster formed and waited patiently for my order. I was very happy that he seemed to have completely recovered from the previous battle.

"Make sure my brothers gather in the castle yard and shut the gates behind them." As soon as the words were out of my mouth, the monster flew out the window and swooped down, herding my brothers through the gates. Only once they were all together in the open did they turn to fight the creature, which had been my intention all along.

When nothing happened, confusion blossomed on their faces. Even though I was far away, I could see their expressions, and I was so pleased for that. The trap Magnus set was pretty much exactly like the one my brothers used on me in Red Rock, except that it worked faster. Instead of draining their magic, it stopped them from using it. If I were to kill them, this would be the time and place to do it, but that was their way of doing things.

That was the sorcerer way.

We all knew the plan. Merlin and Bralyn went outside to fight. I could have turned them invisible, but the spell would have drained off them as soon as they reached my brothers anyway. I didn't worry; although my brothers had swords and knew how to use them, they always relied on their magic. Merlin may have been a wizard trapped in another form, but his wolf form was huge with very sharp claws and teeth. Bralyn had an even greater advantage; he trained his entire life for this kind of battle. Nobody was better with a sword than a warrior.

Since my monkey had so recently been injured and I had confidence in Merlin and Bralyn, I let my monster return to wherever it stayed when it wasn't called.

Magnus and I went to the main room just as Mikron and Thaddeus did. I specifically instructed Merlin and Bralyn to go after my older brothers first for this exact reason. As soon as they were inside, they closed the door and flipped the iron latch into place to keep anyone from following them. That was my brothers; each of them would sacrifice the others to save himself. They spotted me at the same time. Thaddeus looked shocked to see me, but Mikron glared angrily and said, "I knew you came to help the wizard. Mother is going to kill you so painfully."

Thaddeus grabbed the sleeve of Mikron's sorcerer robe to stop him from coming at me. "Wait, maybe he has an explanation." He turned to me and for the first time, there was concern in his eyes. Concern for me. "Explain. Tell me you didn't betray us."

"Betray you? What do you call trying to kill me numerous times in my life? You yourself tried to drown me when I was born."

"Do you really think if I wanted to drown you, you would still be alive? If I hadn't held you underwater in that lake until Father found us, Zeus would have killed you with a rock. It wasn't my fault you were blond. This," he pointed from me to Magnus and back, "is betrayal. We're family; we fight each other, but you went to our enemy. You're no longer family."

"I don't want to be part of a family that drowns its members."

Mikron's anger turned to pure hatred. "You're choosing to conspire with wizards?"

"There is one thing a sorcerer never does, and that is lose. I would rather side with Magnus against you than go back to being your target practice."

216

"Ayden, you can't turn back from this," Thaddeus said, almost pleadingly.

"What did you say to Zeus?" I asked.

"Come back to us and our brothers will never know. We can defeat Magnus together."

"They'll never know?!" Mikron screeched. "I'm telling Zeustrum!"

"No, you won't," Thaddeus said, giving him a look I didn't quite understand. Mikron did apparently, because he snapped his mouth shut. "I can't tell you things will change, but if you fight with us, you'll prove yourself to Mother. If you fight with the wizard, you can never return home. Don't choose this stranger over your family."

"I'm not choosing Magnus over you; I'm choosing to do what I feel is right over sorcery. I've made my choice, and now I'm giving you one. Just you. You gave me the chance to run, so I'm returning the mercy. Run. Run back home, run away, I don't care. Just run from here. There's a back door right down that hall that leads to a forest. Our brothers will never know what happened, and they'll never be able to tell anyone."

"You mean to kill them?"

"We have no mercy; we are sorcerers," Mikron snarled.

"Stop talking," I said. My magic reacted on its own and faster than my brother could retaliate. Blue energy shot into him and his lips sealed like Vactarus's had. "That's better." Thaddeus looked shocked, but also afraid. "This is your only chance. In a moment, Zeus and Bev are going to burst through those doors and you'll face the same fate as them. Run."

He looked from me to Magnus before running into the hall. I heard a back door open.

"Are you sure that was wise?" Magnus asked.

"No, but it was my choice. One act of mercy, followed by five acts of revenge."

Still mute, Mikron pulled out his wand and stomped towards me in anger. Had he been intelligent at all, he would have used his magic and stayed away from me, but Mikron was young and wanted to intimidate me. He froze right in the middle of my painted designs and honest horror came over his face.

He looked down at the designs and tried to step out of the circle, but it was as if there was an invisible barrier keeping him in. In fact, that was exactly what it was; a barrier from another world holding him in place. Any magic he used would be reflected back into himself. Of course, it also released him from my silencing spell. I held my staff outward and focused my energy into the sigils surrounding the circle. When they glowed blue, Mikron panicked. "Wait! Aren't you going to show me mercy? I never tried to kill you!"

"No, you didn't. You just beat me until I couldn't stand. This is merciful."

Magnus's magic joined mine and blazing white and blue magic swirled around the circle like a tornado. Mikron vanished slowly and the magic dispersed. I was merciful because I didn't kill or even injure my brother. Instead, Magnus and I sent him to a world where there was no magic, where Mikron was just a man.

Right on time, the door burst open. Febarin entered, bleeding, panting, and furious. He was even angrier when he saw me with Magnus. He didn't even demand an explanation; he just ran at Magnus with his sword aimed. Obviously, he hadn't realized that he could use magic again. Nevertheless, he ran right into my circle and slammed into the invisible barrier. His sword clattered on the ground and he thrashed and punched the barricade like a caged animal.

"What are you doing, Ayden?! Kill the wizard!"

Without a word, Magnus and I released our magic into the circle and Febarin was still screaming obscenities when he vanished.

"Are you alright?" Magnus asked me, genuine concern in his voice.

I nodded. "Three down, three to go."

At that moment, Zeustrum, Bevras, Gibus, Merlin, and Bralyn burst inside. Merlin and Zeustrum were doing hand-to-paw combat while Gibus and Bralyn were dueling with swords. Bevras started for Magnus, but Gibus broke away from the werebear to intercept Bevras. "Stay away from the circle," he warned. I groaned; Gibus always turned to curses; he would know a magical trap when he saw one.

Bevras aimed his wand and shot black lightning at Magnus. Magnus responded with a white shield of magic around him. He was a wizard; he wouldn't attack first, but that didn't mean he wouldn't strike back. He retaliated with white lightning.

Bralyn shouted when the stone floor began crawling up his legs. The stone was literally spreading as if it was alive, and Bralyn had no idea how to counteract stone. "Shift!" I told him as I turned my focus on helping Merlin. The wolf had bitten a good chunk out of Zeustrum's right arm, but my eldest brother was ambidextrous and took up his sword in his left hand as if he had been born to it. My blue magic covered the blade of his sword and made it grow heavier and heavier as he used it.

Magnus's magic shielded me as Bevras shot some curse at me. It reflected and hit Bralyn who was mauling Gibus. The bear convulsed in pain and collapsed on top of Gibus. I knew it would be a matter of moments before Gibus recovered. Bralyn was still breathing, but he shifted back into his person form. He wasn't that much smaller.

Magnus's white magic wrapped around Bevras and tossed him into the circle. "No!" Zeustrum yelled, abandoning his fight with Merlin to save his twin. Merlin went after him and managed to wrestle him to the ground, but he landed on the outer sigils. Zeus wasn't dumb; he used his sword to scrape two of the sigils even as Merlin was dragging him away. With the symbols ruined, the circle lost its power. Bevras took Zeus's place in fighting Merlin and Zeus flung a spell at Magnus, which the wizard barely managed to block with another shield.

"Repaint the seal!" Magnus said.

I used my magic to make myself invisible and my skin impenetrable, and then grabbed the paints that had been left out of the way beside the staircase. I had to dodge magic, fists, and teeth, but I made it back to the circle without getting injured. Then I hesitated because I didn't remember what the correct sigils were. Suddenly the image of the symbols I had painted appeared in my mind. I knew, somehow, that it was Merlin pushing the memory into my head.

As I repainted the symbols, Magnus covered me from Zeus's attack. Only when I was done did I look up to see Gibus attacking Magnus.

"*Get down!*" Merlin demanded. I did, covering my still-wet symbols. An instant later, Gibus was shoved towards me, tripped over me, and toppled to the ground inside the circle. None of us had seen Bralyn rise. The warrior shifted back into a bear and tossed Zeustrum across the room. Bevras tried to curse Bralyn, but Merlin caught Bevras's wand in his teeth and snapped it in half. Bev screamed in fury, which drew Zeus's attention to him. Zeus tried to get to him, but Bralyn blocked his path.

I picked up my staff, then Magnus and I activated the circle once again. Gibus vanished inside the white and blue magic. I felt the draw on my magic, but my heart was pumping hard enough I didn't think I could rest if I tried. Zeustrum shot lightning at Bralyn and the bear went down. He was out of this fight.

Magnus engaged Zeus and I turned my efforts to helping Merlin. Even though Bevras's wand was broken, he could still do magic and he still had his sword. Fortunately, Merlin seemed to have at least a low-level resistance to magic. I raised my staff and purposefully didn't think of any curse in particular. *Attack*.

That never would have worked if I only had my wand. This time, blue lightning struck my brother in the back. He tensed up and collapsed in what looked like pure agony. If it was anyone else, even Zeustrum, I would have felt pity. I still had scars from Bevras whipping me, though, so I had no sympathy for him.

I barely saw the movement before heavy wings closed over me. The monkey monster made a horrific cry of pain before vanishing. That was when I saw Magnus on the ground. Zeustrum had attacked me and my monster saved my life. I attacked Zeus and he was forced to put a shield over himself, which gave Merlin enough time to drag Bevras towards the circle.

Magnus was getting back to his feet, but he was injured and it was going to take him some time to recover enough to attack. When Bevras was right next to the circle, Merlin backed away. He couldn't get Bevras into it without getting himself trapped. "Merlin, take Zeus," I said. Merlin didn't argue. As soon as he left Bevras's side, I imagined my brother levitating and let my magic do its job. Since he didn't weigh nearly as much as a pirate ship, it was almost easy. My power fled as soon as I pushed him into the circle. He was still unconscious and he was trapped again. I wouldn't let Zeustrum free him this time.

I completely expected Merlin to be able to handle my eldest brother, so when I turned to them, I just froze. There was no instinctive action, epiphany, or even luck on my side this time. Black, glowing bands of magic were wrapped around Merlin's neck and limbs, similar to the restraints I had on my monkey. Only these were meant to kill, not control. He was lying at Zeustrum's feet in obvious pain and Zeustrum held his blade pressed gently against Merlin's throat.

"Drop the staff," Zeus said.

I did. There was nothing I could say to stop him, no secret I could bribe him with, and no doubt he would kill Merlin if the wolf wasn't of more use to him alive. "I can't release Bevras without my staff."

"You will, or the wolf dies. Scuff the sigils."

*"If you do, he will kill me anyway,"* Merlin said.

*"What am I supposed to do? I can't just let him kill you. Tell me what to do."*

*"Follow your heart."*

I slowly approached Bevras. Following my heart was what got me into this mess in the first place. It was so important to me to prove myself to my mother, my brothers, and everyone else. Instead, I proved to myself that I wasn't a sorcerer. No, I wasn't a sorcerer... but I did sort of prove myself in another way.

Magnus, the greatest wizard known, counted on me to save him, and I did. I proved that people could rely on me. I saved the elf king's daughter and proved that I keep my word. I created a monster that could destroy a village and ended up saving them from it, proving that I fixed my mistakes. I joined a wizard's wand and sorcerer's staff, proving that I was something different. Maybe I was a freak, but at least I wasn't like my brothers. I didn't try to kill a wizard just because he existed.

I didn't have enough dark magic to fight Zeustrum, but my wand had shown me that it wasn't really necessary. Saving Merlin was more important than killing Zeus. I focused my mind on what happened so many days ago. It felt like ages ago when I wandered into a little village, trying to make a name for myself. Magic tensed inside me, ready to strike, but not to injure. I remembered my state of mind, my desire, and the sensation of my magic when I turned every sword in an entire village into flowers. Magic released from me, not my wand or staff, and Zeustrum was suddenly holding a bouquet of flowers.

The shock on his face was instantaneous and I used that distraction to reach out my hand and call my staff to me. It leapt up from the ground, across the room, and into my hand. Since Magnus was still disorientated, I poured my magic into the circle. The sigils came alive and blue energy swirled around my unconscious brother.

Fortunately, I didn't have to know anything about the world I was sending him to, because it was the sigils and their arrangement that determined what world the portal opened to. It took longer than with my other brothers because this was just my magic, but eventually, Bevras vanished.

"No!" Zeustrum had his wand in hand when I turned back to him and I could sense the magic swelling inside him.

There was no time to think, no time for defensive magic, and no time to feel regret. There was only the absolute certainty that I was about to die. It would be quick and very painful, and then I would be dead. There was a flash of burning red light.

Zeustrum didn't yell, or even show surprise on his face; he just fell. Behind him, my father stood. I gaped, but he simply pocketed his wand, put his finger to his lips in a gesture of silence, and disappeared.

I had no time to even let the shock settle in because Zeus was still alive. I used levitation on him just like I had on Bevras, but when I finally dropped him in the circle and poured my magic into it, I knew I didn't have enough left in me to send him off.

My heart beat too quickly, my breath was too hard to draw in, and my vision was becoming blurry. I pushed every drop of what I had left into that circle and right before I failed, white energy joined mine in the circle. Magnus was back in the fight. I held on just long enough to see Zeustrum fade out of our existence.

\*       \*       \*

I woke in a soft, comfortable bed. My eyes felt sore, but I opened them anyway. Merlin was curled up on the rug in front of the fireplace. I wondered why Magnus hadn't broken his curse, but the door burst open before I could ask.

Merlin hadn't expected the sound and popped up on all fours with a furious growl. He stopped growling when he realized it was just Bralyn. The werebear grinned at me. "I'm glad to see that you made it."

"I could say the same about you. How long have I been asleep?"

"Just a day. Magnus gave you a healing potion, but---"

"But they don't work on strained magic," I finished, sitting up. "Why are you still here?"

"I just wanted to make sure you survived. I'll be heading back to my guild tonight. Thank you. Shapeshifters make good warriors, but not one who is allergic to fur. With your help, I proved to myself that I am just as good as the rest of them. If you ever need help on another quest, I'll be around." He left.

"Why didn't Magnus break the curse?" I asked.

"*I never told you what Dessa told me when we were alone.*"

"I thought she told you how to break the curse."

"*Not exactly. She told me it would be broken on the day you die.*"

"Seers can get it wrong."

"*I know, but she assured me that is not the case. She could not tell me how or why, and I could not exactly ask her, but she was certain.*"

"That's why you didn't want me to try?"

"*Yes.*"

"Then what are you going to do now?"

"*I realized while fighting your brothers that it is not so bad being a wolf. Yes, I want to have my powers back, but this form is not without its defenses. Furthermore, it is somewhat peaceful. For hundreds of years, my life revolved around magic. Now I realize how tired of it I was. I shall think of this as a vacation.*"

"It'll be a short vacation. My mother will be hunting me down now that my brothers are gone."

"*No, I think not. Your mother only wants you for your power, and as far as she will know, you only have white magic now. Yes, she will eventually seek revenge on you and Magnus, so I highly suggest you stay here at the castle. Magnus has already asked me to relay the offer. You lived your life in dark magic and you have made your choice. Now is your chance to learn light magic. When your mother eventually comes to fight you, you will both stand a better chance together.*"

"What are you going to do?"

"*Well, Magnus has extended the welcome to me and I am strongly considering taking him up on the offer. After all, I still have a thing or two I could teach you.*"

I grinned. "I guess we're going to stay then. The sorcerer who isn't a sorcerer and the wolf who isn't a wolf."

"*Does that still bother you?*"

"No. I think I'm okay. I am who I am."

# EPILOGUE

"I can't believe you had black hair and I missed it," Kisha said.

After a few days at Magnus's castle, I told the old wizard about Vactarus and that I needed to return the magician's hat. Magnus said that he had no idea the hat's owner was still around. He gave me the hat and transported Merlin and me to Vactarus's mansion. I tried to tell him I could just take a ship, but he insisted. Apparently, I would become powerful enough to transport myself that far if I practiced for as long as he had.

Vactarus was overjoyed to have his hat back and offered me any of the leftover stuff left in the mansion. Since I needed more clothes and I really wanted to start my own collection of books, I took him up on the offer. That was how I came to spend five days going through boxes of old junk. Kisha couldn't help sort, but she was fun to talk to. Even if she didn't have memories of her life, she could read books.

"You should write stories that people can read for fun," she suggested thoughtfully.

"Maybe after I see more of the world." I was actually hoping Merlin would take me to see other worlds when we break his curse. Despite the fact that he was willing to wait for my sake, I was determined to find a way to break it without getting myself killed in the process. The first step in doing that was to go back to Dessa and ask her how I'm supposed to die on the day his curse is broken. Unfortunately, the tournament was over and I didn't know how to find her again.

"Hey, I've seen that before," Kisha said, pointing to a small painted wooden doll in a box.

I picked it up and studied it. It was very creepy, especially since it resembled Kisha. In fact, the doll wore a blue dress identical to Kisha's. "I think it's supposed to be you."

"I don't remember it, only that I've seen it before."

The box was full of a young girl's clothes and just one other thing; a drawing of Kisha standing between a man and woman. The disturbing part was that the heads of both the man and woman were cut off.

"What is this?" she asked.

"I think this was a drawing of you and your parents, but maybe someone didn't want anyone to know who your parents were." More likely, whoever killed Kisha had killed her parents or was planning to afterwards. I turned it over to see three names: Magnus Vobristum, Livia Dracre, and Sonya Dracre.

# ABOUT THE AUTHOR

Rain Oxford is a teacher who has been writing for more than half of her life. She does most of her writing in a secluded cabin in the woods with a four-pound Maltese as a companion. When she's not teaching or creating worlds, she usually enjoys cooking, playing the piano, or photographing exotic wildlife.

Made in the USA
Lexington, KY
27 November 2016